"You did that on purpose!"

The camcorder operator moved into position behind Libby, filming Sabrina.

"You're trying to hurt the work everyone has done on this carnival," Sabrina said.

"No, I'm not." Libby was totally cool.

Bob Gordon stood beside the camcorder operator, urging him to move. "This is the kind of stuff we want. The pure essence of what being a teen in today's world is all about. The combativeness, the rivalry for attention and control, all the angst."

"Sabrina, everything I've done has been to promote the Harvest Moon Dance," Libby said. "That's what this carnival is all about, right?"

"No, it's about everybody coming together to work for something they wanted."

"What *they* wanted?" Libby asked. "Or what *you* wanted? I don't think you've taken a good look at your own agenda lately."

Libby walked away. Channel Eight followed her, the camcorder operator getting final footage of Sabrina standing in stunned silence.

Sabrina, the Teenage Witch™ books

Available from ARCHWAY Paperbacks

Sabrina The Teenage Witch™

Harvest Moon

Mel Odom

AN ARCHWAY PAPERBACK
Published by POCKET BOOKS
New York London Toronto Sydney Tokyo Singapore

AN ARCHWAY PAPERBACK *Original*

An Archway Paperback published by
POCKET BOOKS, a division of Simon & Schuster Inc.
1230 Avenue of the Americas, New York, NY 10020

ISBN: 0-671-02119-2

First Archway Paperback printing November 1998

10 9 8 7 6 5 4 3 2 1

AN ARCHWAY PAPERBACK and colophon are
registered trademarks of Simon & Schuster Inc.

SABRINA THE TEENAGE WITCH and all related titles, logos
and characters are trademarks of Archie Comics Publications, Inc.

Printed in the U.S.A.

IL: 4+

Harvest Moon

☆

Chapter 1

☆

"**S**abrina Spellman, what do you think you're doing?"

Aunt Zelda's reproach, delivered with the max in authority, let Sabrina know she was in mondo trouble.

"It's not what you think," Sabrina said weakly. Then she remembered how much she hated starting out any kind of defense with those words.

Zelda Spellman stood in the doorway leading out to the living room. Her short blond hair framed her face and lay precisely in place. She stared at her niece over her reading glasses, the forefinger of one hand stuck into a fat copy of *Tuttleby's Crescent Wrench for Quantum Mechanics Everywhere*. "There is no reason for scrying on someone." She walked into the room

1

and looked at the contents of the bowl on the kitchen counter. She waved an arm.

Obediently the water rose from the bowl in a column spread out as big as a basketball. The increase in size and viewing area made Sabrina feel even more guilty for scrying, spying on someone by casting a spell across the surface of a body of water. In this case, Salem's water bowl.

"Actually," Aunt Hilda said as she entered the room behind Zelda, "there was a reason for scrying at one time." Blond as her sister, the resemblance almost stopped there. Hilda was a free spirit, and it showed in the unruly curls and mischievous, dimpled smile she habitually wore. "Before telecommunications and cellular phones, scrying was actually quite helpful."

Zelda cut her sister off immediately. "I'd hate to have to be the one to explain to her father how she came to be fined by the Witches' Council for invasion of privacy. She hasn't even received her witch's license yet."

A troubled expression took some of the zing out of Hilda's dimpled smile. "I'm afraid that's true, sweetheart. Whatever possessed you to scry on anyone? And who is it?"

"Hilda!" Zelda remonstrated.

"Well," Hilda retorted with a brief flush of embarrassment, pulling away from the water, "it does make you kind of curious, doesn't it?"

Sabrina wanted to scream. "I wasn't scrying

on anyone," she stated again, and this time she found she was trying to convince herself as well. "I was just making sure everything is going okay at the carnival. There are so many things we need to get done in the next two days."

Hilda peered more closely at the twisting water. "This *does* look like the school gym."

Zelda looked as well, then shook her head. "That's beside the point," she announced as she waved her hand. The swirling water in the bowl leaped into the sink and gurgled down the drain. "Did you know the risks you were taking? There are several reasons why scrying isn't allowed."

Sabrina knew that. Since her sixteenth birthday, when her father had taken her to live with his sisters, she'd started learning the rules concerning witches and the things they could do with their magic. That was the day she'd learned she was a witch herself, gifted with amazing powers. Hilda and Zelda counseled her on her newly discovered abilities as well as the responsibilities they expected her to learn to assume. Especially the responsibility part.

"I know why it isn't allowed." Sabrina sighed, feeling lower than low. "It's not polite." She crossed to the kitchen table and sat, ready to listen to the coming lecture.

"As well as demeaning and potentially harmful," Zelda pointed out. "Even to a good relationship."

"I wasn't scrying on Harvey," Sabrina explained, knowing her aunt had gotten the wrong impression. Harvey Kinkle was her semiofficial boyfriend, and she'd already learned the wisdom of leaving their relationship in the hands of true love.

"Scrying wasn't so bad before colonial America," Hilda put in, peering briefly into the refrigerator, then emerging with a frown. "Why, back in the Middle Ages, the occasional glimpse of a loved one or an enemy in a bowl of frankincense or wine helped a witch achieve a certain social standing."

"Not to mention a position of financial gain," Salem observed. He rubbed his paws together at a fond memory. "I can remember how appreciative the De Medicis were."

"But scrying is now against the Witches' Code of Ethics," Zelda said, "so I'd like an explanation."

"It's the carnival," Sabrina answered, feeling the pressure and frustration settle heavily on her. "If it doesn't earn the money we need for the Harvest Moon Dance, there won't be a Harvest Moon Dance." She hated putting the possibility into words. It felt like such a jinx.

Since she'd found out she was a witch, some of the things she'd considered part of normal everyday life seemed to be just out of reach. Like holidays. Her parents' divorce had changed her home life in that regard as well.

That was why the Harvest Dance at Westbridge High School was tremendously important to her, and why she'd volunteered for the job of overseeing the carnival to fund the dance.

"I just wanted to make sure everything was going okay at the gym," Sabrina went on. "So I peeked."

"You could have been there instead of here," Zelda said. "You could zap back and forth. Of course, you'd want to be careful about that, too."

"I *was* there instead of here," Sabrina replied, indicating the old jeans and chambray work shirt she had on. She didn't really have any old clothes, thanks to her powers, so she'd had to point herself up some. "I zapped myself home for only an instant. Just long enough to try to get a little quiet time to myself and grab a snack."

"Oh, Sabrina," Hilda said, patting her niece on the hand. "We've seen how you've been worrying yourself these last few days, but we can help if you let us."

"You've been quite adamant about doing this by yourself," Zelda agreed.

"The Harvest Moon Dance is for the student body, and *they* should be the ones helping put the carnival together."

"But they aren't," Salem said. "Ingrates. We should give them a piece of—"

Zelda froze the cat into silence with a glare.

"Or not," Salem said.

"I guess I'm not the inspirational leader I

5

thought I could be," Sabrina said. "If Libby Chessler had managed the carnival, more people would have gotten involved."

Libby Chessler was one of Sabrina's least favorite people at the high school. As head cheerleader for Westbridge, Libby garnered plenty of attention. She also wore the latest expensive fashions, bragged about the social connections her family had, and absolutely controlled who made the Who's Who list of popularity at school.

"You don't know that," Zelda said.

"Yes, I do," Sabrina said. "You wouldn't believe how many people have asked me over the last two weeks why Libby isn't running things."

"How are things going with the carnival?" Zelda asked.

"We're behind," Sabrina admitted. "Getting everything set up is more of a problem. The lumber we needed to make the booths only arrived this afternoon. Today is Thursday, and tomorrow night is the last night before the carnival. The way I'd planned it, we'd have everything done by tonight."

"Won't anyone help out tomorrow?"

"A few of the kids," Sabrina said. "But it's Friday night and they have dates. *I* have a date. With Harvey. I don't want to miss that."

"The dance is a date as well, isn't it?" Zelda asked.

Sabrina experienced a sinking feeling. "This is going to be one of those Life's Lessons Lectures, isn't it? About commitment and the big picture?"

"Afraid so," Zelda said. "If the dance doesn't come off, what are you going to tell all the people who've donated prizes to the carnival? What are you going to tell the people who've already bought tickets to the carnival?"

"I know," Sabrina said. "When no one offered to get the carnival organized, I couldn't believe it. I mean, coming right before Thanksgiving and Christmas as it is, the dance gives everybody one last chance for a party before things get really hectic for the holidays."

"Then I'd say it's up to you to make sure it happens," Zelda pointed out.

"I know."

"And we'll help," Hilda promised.

"I know. Thanks, guys." Sabrina looked at Zelda. "And I'm sorry about the scrying, but I feel like I can't take my eyes off things for even a minute."

"Do what you can," Zelda suggested, "and trust that everything will work out."

Sabrina nodded agreeably, but worry clouded her mind anyway. The carnival was such a big commitment, and she had such high hopes for it. But canceling a date with Harvey was no fun at all. Depressed and unable to see that silver lining

Hilda was always talking about, she zapped herself back to the gym.

How could something so potentially cool as the Harvest Moon Dance turn into such a headache? Sabrina stared at the chaos spreading out across the gym floor as her best friend Valerie Birckhead came over. Most of it was caused by the thirty volunteers she'd managed to gather. It was hard to imagine the tiny town of carnival booths set up and ready to go any time soon.

"We're not going to be finished tonight," she told Valerie. "We're going to need to work tomorrow night."

Disbelief covered Valerie's face. "But, Sabrina, that's Friday night!" Normally well dressed and groomed, Valerie wore stained jeans and a flannel shirt tied at the waist. Wisps of dark hair hung down into her face.

"I know," Sabrina replied glumly. "I've got a date with Harvey."

"I've got a—" Valerie looked uncertain. "Well, it's Friday night. I at least usually put in an appearance at the Slicery before I go home and feel sorry for myself." Though Valerie actually was a very cute girl, her romantic life never seemed to do more than fizzle. The Slicery was the pizza parlor hangout for most of the students of Westbridge. "What about Saturday morning? We could come in early and finish it then."

"We're planning on taking food deliveries and finishing the prep work then. Do you think we're going to have any extra time?"

It only took Valerie a moment to arrive at a conclusion. "Not really."

"Neither do I." Sabrina gazed around the gym and felt hopelessly outnumbered. If she could use her magic, she could have the gym ready for the carnival in minutes.

And if I do, she thought, *what do I tell everybody? That the cobbler's elves must have taken the night off and took pity on a bunch of struggling teenagers trying to put a fund-raising carnival together?*

Her mind stayed busy, sorting through all the details as she and Valerie took a tour around the gym floor. Areas were marked off for the basketball and dart-throwing competitions, for the Knock 'em Down softball throw, for the archery competition (although the arrows had rubber suction cups instead of sharp tips), and the football toss. Other sections had been set aside for the Weight/Age Guesstimation, temporary tattoos, face-painting, caricature drawing, the dunking tank, and the various food booths. It was a lot crammed into a small space, but Sabrina had wanted to put as many events as possible in the carnival.

Overhead, some of the volunteers conversed in loud voices, alternately laughing and joking, then growing frustrated with their efforts at spreading out the booth tents. The colorful material hung like dead mushrooms.

Sabrina looked at the banner at the opposite end of the gym. She hadn't noticed when it had gone up, though it had been ready for the last two days.

WELCOME TO WESTBRIDGE CARNIVAL! the green banner read in big white letters. ALL PROCEEDS AND DONATIONS GO TO THE WESTBRIDGE HARVEST MOON DANCE! THANKS FOR YOUR HELP!

A poster drawn in colorful markers hung below it. On the poster an astronaut danced with a two-headed green alien in a sparkly area that looked like the Milky Way. At least, it was supposed to look like the Milky Way. Actually it looked like a pink cloud of silvery sparkles.

GO OUT OF THIS WORLD AT THE WESTBRIDGE HARVEST MOON DANCE! read the caption under the poster.

The concept for the dance was Sabrina's idea, too. Rather than sticking with a traditional seasonal theme, scarecrows and pumpkins—and someone had even mentioned the possibility of a *Wizard of Oz* theme because of the scarecrow character—Sabrina had chosen a space theme. Attendees could come as the science-fiction character of their choice.

The dance was going to take place at Happy's Ice Rink in downtown Westbridge. A down payment for the rink rental had been taken out of the advance carnival ticket sales. Those sales had been pretty dismal, though, and if the carnival didn't make a decent amount of money Saturday night, the ice rink wouldn't be reserved. Neither would the catering service or the special effects Sabrina was counting on to make the dance a success.

"You're going to have to break it to them," Valerie said, bringing Sabrina's mind back to the current problem.

"Break what to who?" a pleasant male voice asked.

Sabrina's heart beat a little faster when she recognized the voice. She turned and spotted Harvey coming toward her. Just seeing him made her feel better and put a smile on her face.

Harvey still wore his football practice clothes, the white pants with grass stains that almost matched his green jersey. His sandy brown hair was still damp from practice. He wasn't first-string for the Fighting Scallions football team, and rarely got off the bench during a game, but he put his heart into everything he did.

That was only one of the reasons Sabrina liked him.

"Hi, Harvey," Sabrina said.

"Hi, Sab," he said with a smile, using his pet name for her. "Why do you look so stressed out?"

"Because she *is* stressed out," Valerie informed him. "Does this carnival look ready to you?"

Harvey looked around. "It's not as far along as I would have thought," he admitted.

Sabrina knew he was being generous. *He's probably thinking Libby could have done a better job at getting things organized, too.* The thought made her angry and sad all at the same time. "The lumber suppliers didn't bring any nails for the booths."

Harvey dropped his football equipment bag on the floor. "I'll go over to the lumberyard and get the nails. We'll build what we can tonight, then finish up tomorrow."

"Tomorrow's Friday," Valerie pointed out.

Harvey looked troubled. "I forgot." He turned to Sabrina. "How would you feel about spending our date here?"

And that was another reason Sabrina liked Harvey so much. "You don't mind?" she asked.

"Sab," he said, "I know how much Harvest Moon Dance means to you. I don't mind spending the time here tomorrow." He paused. "I mean, if you're okay with that?"

"Harvey Kinkle," Sabrina said, giving him a brief hug, "you are truly fab!"

Released, Harvey blushed scarlet. "We can split a pizza at the Slicery, or we can get a pizza delivered. As long as we're together, that's all that matters, right?"

"Right. And that gives me a great idea!"

Wanting to strike while she had the courage, Sabrina went to the announcer's desk at half-court. She turned on the PA system, cringing as the electronic squeal echoed through the gym.

All the volunteers stopped what they were doing, lowered the volume on their boom boxes, and turned to face her.

"I've got a big favor to ask," Sabrina said. "It doesn't take a rocket scientist to see that we're not going to finish with the carnival booths tonight."

The assents from the crowd of volunteers were equal to the groans from those who'd figured out what was coming.

"We don't want to have to come back tomorrow night and do this," someone from the group bellowed. A chorus of agreement sounded immediately.

Maybe the cobbler's elves stories could *work,* Sabrina thought. *Maybe everybody wants out of the extra work enough that* no one *would ask questions.* "I know Friday night is a big night for all of us. Harvey and I had a date planned, but we're going to be here tomorrow evening. I'd appreciate any of you who could to come out tomorrow."

There was more muttering, but from what Sabrina could hear, it was in her favor. "Tomorrow night doesn't have to be a complete bummer," she went on. "Why don't we pool our money together and have the Slicery deliver pizza and drinks? That way we can kind of have a pre-party."

Enthusiastic whistles and shouts punctuated the positive support of the idea.

Sabrina switched the PA system off, and Harvey helped her down. "That is a cool idea, Sab," he said.

"Actually," she told him, "the idea was yours. I just moved it to a bigger scale. You're going to get the nails, right?"

"Color me gone," Harvey responded. "I'll be back as soon as I can." He jogged off.

Sabrina turned to Valerie. "Why don't we make a final list of the things that still need doing?"

"Making a list of the things that have already been done would probably be shorter," her friend said.

Sabrina led the way, trying not to get overwhelmed or depressed by how much remained to be done. While she was working in the food area, laying out the placement of the booths and what they'd need to stock in the way of condiments and disposable silverware, she saw Libby Chessler enter the gym with two men following her.

Dark haired and slim, dressed in a tangerine-colored minidress, a chocolate-colored turtleneck, and a matching tangerine short-waisted jacket, Libby looked stunning amid all the carnival volunteers. She waved condescendingly to a couple of people who called out to her, but she never stopped talking to the men behind her.

Sabrina recognized one of the men as Bob Gordon, the Eyewitness Action News Center Eight newsman. He'd also been the judge at a cat show where Sabrina had won first place. As a cat. He wore a blue suit that looked surprisingly good on him and nodded a lot while Libby talked.

The other man carried a camcorder over one shoulder that sprayed out a cone of light over the gym floor. He wore a T-shirt and jeans.

"Curious, isn't it?" Valerie asked as they watched Libby.

"I'd call it hypnotic," Sabrina replied. "Kind of like watching a shark's dorsal fin break water at the beach." She didn't know what Libby was doing at the gym, but she was willing to bet it wasn't for any good reason.

Chapter 2

Throwing a 'pre-carnival party' is truly the sign of a desperate mind, Sabrina."

Recognizing Libby Chessler's voice, Sabrina bit back a scathing retort and concentrated instead on pressing the poster she'd made for the party against the wall. The masking-tape loops on the back would hold it in place.

The sign read like a newspaper's headlines: HARVEST MOON DANCE BENEFIT CARNIVAL'S SUCCESS SPURS SPIN-OFF PARTY! Smaller letters below stated: LOOKING FOR A PLACE TO REALLY LET THE HAMMER DOWN? COME TO THE WESTBRIDGE HIGH GYM AT 7:00 P.M. TONIGHT TO SEE THOSE WHO SAW!

Finished with the sign, Sabrina spun around to face Libby. "There are some of us who believe in the carnival and want the dance."

Libby looked like a Hollywood star in an off-the-shoulder copper-colored wrap dress that had a metallic green weave worked into it. Her dark hair fell perfectly into place and dark wrap-around Foster Grant sunglasses covered her eyes. She'd even found shoes to match the dress.

"You mean the Dance of the Dead?" Libby taunted. "Brought to you by the carnival that hasn't been built?"

Cee Cee and Jill and a few of the other cheerleaders stood behind Libby.

"I recall," Sabrina said, "that you weren't in favor of a Harvest Moon Dance. You were going to have a party at your house with a few of your closest friends."

"I changed my mind. And obviously that was a Good Thing. Otherwise even the coolest people would be subjected to your lame-o planning." Libby turned to the group of cheerleaders behind her and pressed the backs of her hands against her forehead. She curled her fingers dramatically. "Not everyone looks good in tentacles, you know."

The cheerleaders laughed with the same kind of precision they would have if Libby had held up a prompt card.

Actually, Sabrina thought, *the tentacled look could become permanent, Libby. All it would require is one little point.* The teenage witch placed her hands behind her back to push away the temptation to point and make it happen.

"Not everyone's coming in tentacles," Sabrina retorted. "I'll bet there are still a few slime-creature costumes out there you can get your hands on."

"Save your carnival if you want," Libby replied shortly. "I always say, why send in a real person to do a clown's job? And even if you do save the carnival by some divine miracle, that doesn't mean the dance will be yours."

Sabrina started to argue and tell Libby that she'd never considered the dance to be hers to begin with. But she resisted and kept moving. There were still a lot of posters to be put up.

Thankfully, Libby found someone else to torture, calling out in a loud voice. The cheerleaders trailed after her like ducklings.

Sabrina plastered another sign by the media center door. The five-minute warning bell sounded with a strident shriek. She rolled the remaining posters together but couldn't manage to tie the shoestring around them.

"I've got it," Valerie said, coming up behind Sabrina. Valerie put her bookbag down and picked up the shoestring. "I saw Libby and her crew talking to you. Were they bad?" She finished tying the shoestring.

"It's early," Sabrina answered. "They haven't been awake long enough to figure out how to be truly wicked."

"The job Libby's got at 2 Chic By Design has inflated her already overinflated ego." Valerie helped Sabrina stuff the roll of posters into her locker.

Libby's part-time job was modeling clothes for the mall boutique for the Christmas season. Channel Eight carried the ads during the Saturday night schlock horror film from eleven P.M. to one A.M. Between sessions of monsters and madmen killing teens with cheesy special effects, Libby showed off the latest designs. The ads had been successful enough that other businesses were starting to cater to the teen market with models of their own. But none of the other ads got quite the attention that the 2 Chic By Design Girl did. Sabrina had heard one of the Channel Eight newscasters mention that during a newscast last week.

"Did you ever hear what Libby was doing at the gym last night?" Sabrina asked.

Valerie shook her head, hurrying down the hall to Mr. Pool's science class. "No. Did you?"

"No." Sabrina hurried after her friend, remembering Libby's parting shot about the dance not remaining hers. She hadn't a clue what Libby meant by that, but it left an unsettling cold slither running rampant down her spine.

"Hey, Sab, wait up!"

Hearing Harvey's voice, Sabrina turned around in the cafeteria, nearly jostling the trays from two boys' hands. Lunch was in full swing, filled with flashing serving utensils and loud

conversation. She held an apple in one hand and
the roll of posters tucked under her arm.

"Hi, Harvey," she said.

"Hi, yourself. I thought we were going to eat
together today. Where's your lunch?"

Sabrina held up the apple. "You're looking at
it."

"You don't need to diet, Sab. You look great."

"Thanks. But this isn't about a diet." Sabrina
lifted the roll of posters. "I didn't get a chance to
finish putting the posters out this morning, so I
thought I'd take lunch break and try to get them
all done."

"Could you use some help?"

A warm glow suffused Sabrina. "Oh, Harvey, I
couldn't ask you to give up lunch."

Harvey shrugged. "I won't be giving up lunch.
Maybe a few fries, but definitely not lunch." He
placed his tray on the edge of a table and took
the cheeseburger, chocolate chip cookies, and
carrot sticks. The cookies and carrot sticks
found a new home in his shirt pocket, which was
lined with the paper napkin from the tray. He
held up the cheeseburger. "I can eat this on the
way."

"Thanks. Valerie has taken some posters, too,
so we should have the whole campus covered for
the afternoon."

"Cool. I also have the names of some guys
who'll be able to help us put the booths together." Harvey lunged back to the tray for his
chocolate milk carton, then held it up. "Got

milk." He smiled. "These aren't people who were there last night. I figured all of them would be back, so asking people who hadn't been there only made sense."

Sabrina watched him inhale the cheeseburger as she led the way through the cafeteria doors. She thought it was gone in about four bites, and there wasn't even a drop of ketchup on his chin. "I borrowed my aunts' car to drive down to Happy's after school to pay the down payment on the special-effects gear. Want to come?"

"Want to," Harvey replied, "but can't. We don't have a game tonight because this is a bye week, but Coach is going to have us out in the field for a while anyway. Drills, endurance. That whole pain-is-gain thing. Let me know how it went when you get back?"

"Sure."

Sabrina got back to the gym at twenty minutes to five after stopping by her aunts' house. She fully expected to be the only one there. Instead, she found Harvey and eight more football players already at work putting the booths together. The irregular rhythm of hammers falling mixed with the thunder of rock-and-roll music and filled the gym with noise.

Dressed in jeans and a navy muscle shirt, his face gleaming with perspiration, Harvey glanced up at Sabrina. A broad smile pulled at his lips. Sawdust speckled his features. "Hey, Sab. How does it look?" He waved a hand at the line of booths the boys had built.

The white wood was clean and sturdy, and the booths looked quite capable. All that was needed were the cloth tents to give them some color.

"They look great, Harvey. But what are you guys doing here?"

Harvey shrugged. "We finished up practice, took a shower, and thought we'd go ahead and get started."

"Yeah," Isaac Pierce called out as he held a plywood section while another football player nailed it into place, "the more time we save now, the more time we have for the pre-carnival party tonight."

The other football players hooted in agreement.

"Thanks, guys," Sabrina said, "but if I could borrow a couple volunteers, my aunts baked some snacks for later. They're out in the back of the car."

Harvey and two other boys followed Sabrina out to the car and helped bring in the cakes and cookies her aunts had sent.

"Wow, Sabrina," Todd Jackson said as he toted in a large container of chocolate chip cookies, "your aunts must have been up half the night baking."

No, Sabrina thought, *but there was that frantic half-hour of pointing this afternoon.*

Harvey and Isaac created a makeshift table of plywood across a trio of sawhorses. Then Sabrina spread the snacks across it.

"You're going to need a guard posted to keep hands off the goodies," Isaac said. He studied the line of pies, cakes, and candied apples appreciatively.

"If we eat it all," Sabrina promised, "my aunts said they'd bring more."

"Those are the kind of aunts to have."

Sabrina silently agreed. Hilda and Zelda had even managed to round up a number of the prizes to be given away at the carnival the next night.

Taking out the schedule she'd worked up with Valerie, Sabrina started passing out assignments to the arriving volunteers. When it got to be five o'clock, stragglers were still coming, but there was no sign of Valerie.

There were a lot of questions and additional instructions given, which stressed Sabrina's time majorly. Still, she managed to keep up with all the demands without totally wigging out.

Working in teams, the volunteers lowered the cloth tents over the booth frames. It was amazing how quickly the whole carnival started to take shape, like a small city rising from the polished floor.

Lynne Addams, the dance treasurer, came by with her report on the funding at twenty minutes after five. She was a thin girl with plain looks who knew how to show off her best feature, which was her jade green eyes. She was a top accounting student, and helped do some of the bookkeeping in her father's consulting service. "It doesn't look good, Sabrina," she confided, handing over a computer printout of her treasurer's report. "Unless we do fantastic business at the gate tomorrow night, we're going to be *waaay* short of what we need."

"I know," Sabrina said. She quickly scanned the single-page report.

Lynne had all the figures in black on white, and the columns were very simplified. The profit, even after all the donations, was nowhere near what they needed to put on the Harvest Moon Dance. Sabrina's spirits sank.

"It looks bad, I know," Lynne said, "but it's going to get better."

"Is it?" Sabrina asked.

"Yes, it is," Valerie announced as she came over to join them. She glanced at Sabrina. "Sorry I'm late, but I'm late for a good reason."

"Okay," Sabrina said, struggling not to sound too down over the pathetic profits.

"Remember how we were curious about what Libby was doing here last night?" Valerie asked.

"You found out?" Sabrina asked.

"Yeah, and you're not going to believe it. Our money problems for the dance may be over. And it's all because of Libby Chessler!"

"How is Libby supposed to solve the money problems for the dance?" Sabrina asked.

"I was on my way over here," Valerie said, "when I saw Libby getting filmed with Bob Gordon the Channel Eight news anchor out in front of the school."

"So what was it all about?" Lynne asked.

"I didn't get all of it. But I did overhear Bob Gordon tell Libby that if his producers liked the idea, there could be some major funding for the project."

"For the project?" Sabrina repeated. "But he didn't say anything about the dance?"

"No."

Sabrina breathed a silent sigh of relief. Libby's parting shot from the morning still buzzed in her brain. *That doesn't mean the dance is going to be yours.* That had definitely been a threat. Of some kind.

"Libby brought up the dance," Valerie said. "She said that it was going to be a big deal at the school, and that it was something they'd need to discuss with Bob Gordon's producers because it could be a hot segment."

"A segment of what?" Lynne asked.

Valerie shrugged. "I don't know. About that time Bob Gordon took Libby by the arm, and they got into one of the television vans. I saw how late it was and got over here as quickly as I could."

"They could have been filming another commercial," Sabrina said.

"A fashion commercial in front of Westbridge High?" Valerie shook her head. "No way."

"You're probably right," Sabrina admitted reluctantly. "Whatever Libby's got on her conniving little mind, we'll deal with it when it comes up. In the meantime, let's deal with this carnival." Still, getting her mind to let go of the possible answers for Libby's actions was a difficult task.

"Hey, I think I found another act you can put into the carnival." Harvey helped put a section of plywood into place, then held it as another boy hammered nails into it.

"Where am I going to put it?" Sabrina asked, dodging to one side as another mushroom of cloth descended on a finished booth. "We don't have all the booths finished now."

"If you can talk Jeremy Hiller into doing it," Harvey said, "he could work off a table."

"What kind of act?" Sabrina asked, interested in spite of her problems because of the gleam in Harvey's eyes.

"One of the coolest," Harvey replied. "Jeremy does fortune-telling."

"You mean, like with a crystal ball?"

The other boy finished nailing his end of the plywood. "No," Harvey said around a mouthful of nails as he started hammering them into the section of wood at his end. "I mean like with tarot cards."

Sabrina was familiar with the tarot deck. Even before she'd gone to live with her aunts, a couple of kids at her old school had goofed around with the cards. Suddenly an image of Jeremy Hiller dressed up in a wizard's robe and pointed hat filled her mind. His appearance near the center of the carnival might set the tone for the whole event. "That could be really cool."

"That's what I thought," Harvey said. "I told him I was surprised he hadn't offered to be part of the carnival."

"Would he?"

"Yeah, I think so. A lot of people have always considered Jeremy a real nerdbomb because he was so skinny and short. But last summer, Jeremy grew seven inches and put on forty pounds. If anybody still thinks he's a nerdbomb, they're not telling him about it now."

Sabrina remembered. Jeremy's growth spurt had been part of the gossip that had raced through Westbridge right after the return from summer break. But all that had really happened had been a shift in the regular pecking order.

She'd always found Jeremy to be a nice guy, a little on the shy side, though. "This might be a little attention-intense for Jeremy," Sabrina pointed out.

Harvey shrugged and took another nail from his mouth. "All you can do is ask. But he's done a lot of readings for the guys on the team. When you put those cards in his hands, he gets comfortable."

"Jeremy, do you have a minute?"

Standing on a step ladder, his hands full of the netting he was hanging around the fast-pitch baseball area, Jeremy looked down at Sabrina. He was six-feet-two now, and broad shouldered. He wore his black hair long and curly, and his eyes behind his glasses were pale blue. He wore jeans and a T-shirt with a winged Pegasus and sword-carrying woman dressed in a chain-mail bikini riding it. Some things about Jeremy hadn't changed at all.

"Sure," he answered in a voice that was much deeper than Sabrina remembered.

"Wow, I don't guess I've talked to you lately. I've seen you in the halls, but I don't remember you being this tall."

Jeremy grinned and pushed his glasses up his nose. He pointed down. "Part of it's the stepladder."

"Right. I was just talking to Harvey, and he told me you do tarot card readings."

"Do you want a reading on how well the carnival is going to do?" Jeremy hung the netting to one side and took a plastic-encased deck of cards from his back jeans pocket.

"That's not what I had in mind. How would you like to be in the carnival?"

"Reading fortunes?"

Sabrina smiled. "Exactly. See, you're doing it already."

Jeremy shook his head. "I don't know, Sabrina. I really don't like a whole lot of attention."

"Harvey tells me you've been doing readings already. Those wouldn't be that much different from telling fortunes at the carnival tomorrow night."

"I've been doing them mostly for friends. That's a big difference."

"Okay," Sabrina said, giving in. "Maybe it is a little different. But it's also a way to get a lot of girls in a one-on-one conversation. Well, gotta go." She turned and started to walk away.

"Uh, Sabrina?"

Got ya! Struggling to keep the smile from her face, Sabrina turned back to Jeremy. "Yes?"

"Girls?" Jeremy said, color rising to his face.

"Sure. They always want the dish on the future." Sabrina wasn't proof against that wish herself.

"Maybe I need to rethink my answer."

"Okay." Sabrina started to walk away again.

"Wait!" Jeremy called. "Where are you going?"

"Back to work," Sabrina answered. "You can give me your answer when you know."

"The answer is yes."

"Terrific," Sabrina said, wheeling on him.

Jeremy had that deer-in-the-headlights look. "I hope."

"You'll be great."

"I'm glad one of us thinks so." Jeremy didn't look convinced at all.

Sabrina waved the comment away. "You're in good hands. Just trust me. I've got a costume at home that should fit you just fine." *Or at least it will when I get through zapping it up for you.* It was something she'd seen in the dungeon beneath the Spellman home during one of Zelda's family cleanup days.

"A costume?"

"Yes, a costume. You've got to look the part of the All-Knowing, All-Seeing, Mysterious . . ." Sabrina waited, but nothing came immediately to mind. *". . . Somebody."*

"Somebody?"

"I'll figure out a name, too," Sabrina promised.

"Now I'm really confident."

Feeling better for the small triumph, Sabrina walked back toward Harvey, intending to thank him for the tip. Having a fortune-teller could add dramatically to the carnival. Along the way she came up with a quick spell to aid the volunteers hammering the booths together.

"Hammer one and hammer two,
Nails go in straight and true."

At once the volunteers using the hammers started driving nails home like accomplished journeymen carpenters. As tired as they were, Sabrina didn't think they'd notice how much better they were getting. And if they did, maybe they'd chalk it up to all the experience they were getting tonight.

Checking her watch, she found it was time to call for the pizzas they'd ordered. She and Valerie had collected money earlier, then placed the order. Valerie had gone to the Slicery more than an hour ago to pay in advance.

As she approached the pay phone in the hallway outside the gym, Sabrina spotted Libby Chessler walking toward the main doors through the glass. Bob Gordon and a Channel Eight film crew followed her, trailed by nearly thirty more people.

The camcorder operator swept along in Libby's wake, filming away furiously.

"Hello, tentacle-head," Libby said in a low voice as she walked in front of Sabrina. "Get ready for some really *baaad* news about that precious little party you've got planned, because I'm taking that production over as of right now. You are *so* over!"

Chapter 3

☆

Abandoning the idea of calling the Slicery for the moment, Sabrina walked back into the gym after Libby and the Channel Eight crew. She stood with her back to the wall as Libby pointed out all the booths, obviously giving the television people a tour of the carnival's offerings.

Bob Gordon looked really excited, talking in quick asides to the cameraman and the other production people. The cameraman kept the camcorder on Libby while others took down notes at Bob Gordon's direction.

Sabrina pointed at Libby and Bob Gordon, casting a spell so that she could hear every word they said. It wasn't really eavesdropping, since Libby and the reporter were speaking in a public forum.

"The carnival will be good for the initial

segment," Bob Gordon was saying. He waved at the booths. "We can show how hard the student body here at Westbridge High has tried to put this dance together, how close they've come, only to fall short." He glanced from the booths to Libby. "They are going to fall short, aren't they?"

"Horribly short," Libby answered.

"Well," Bob Gordon said, "that's too bad for them, but it could be a great story for us."

Sabrina went livid with anger. It was everything she could do to keep her pointing finger in check.

Valerie walked over to Sabrina from the crowd. Valerie's expression was one of shock and disbelief. "I've seen Libby do some mean-spirited things, but I never thought I'd see her sink this low. This makes me want to barf."

"You're relatively new to the spectacle," Sabrina told her, referring to the fact that Valerie hadn't been at Westbridge as long as she had. "Libby has depths that I suspect haven't even been plumbed by your garden-variety bottom-feeder before." She started across the gym floor.

"What are you doing?" Valerie asked.

"Trying to keep from turning Libby into something positively icky."

"What?"

"I mean I'm going to try to find out what Libby's doing here."

"Oh. That's what I thought you said."

Cee Cee and Jill saw Sabrina and tried to intercept her. Without being seen, Sabrina pointed at the booth material hanging overhead, then zapped it free of the support wire. The red and gold material fluttered down like a giant jellyfish over both girls. One of them tripped on the material, causing the other to lose her footing as well. They went down in a heap, tangled in the loose cloth.

"I think we need to get a few shots of you working on one of these booths," Bob Gordon was saying when Sabrina arrived.

Libby asked one of the nearest volunteers for his hammer.

"The rest of you people hold up all that hammering and banging for just a few minutes," Bob Gordon requested. "We want to make sure we can hear Libby."

Now that's the last straw, Sabrina thought. *It's one thing—a very bad thing—to come in and start taking credit for the carnival, but it's something else to come in and put us even further behind schedule.* She forced her way through the crowd around Libby and the television newspeople.

"Okay, Libby," the news anchorman said, "give me the story. Tell me about the carnival and about the dance."

"Well, Bob," Libby said, "the student body here at Westbridge High School got together a

34

few weeks ago and decided to have a Harvest Moon Dance."

Sabrina found her way blocked momentarily by a couple of stocky football players. "Excuse me," she said. They parted before her, but it was like working against a river current. More and more people were starting to crowd around Libby and Bob Gordon, drawn by the television cameras. Sabrina chafed with frustration as she continued forward.

"But this is the party season," Bob Gordon said. "Why would you want another party now?"

"You're talking about Thanksgiving and Christmas, right?" Libby tapped on a nail, driving it into the wood in three strokes thanks to Sabrina's spell. "Those are traditionally *family*-oriented holidays. Not ones that the students here can generally spend with our friends."

"She's stealing your speech," Valerie whispered in Sabrina's ear. "That's the same reason you used when you brought it before the school administration."

"And that was what compelled you to push for the Harvest Moon Dance?" Bob Gordon asked.

Sabrina glanced ahead through the crowd. Only another two or three people and she'd be there.

"Yes," Libby said, turning to face the camera. "That and the great new wardrobe from 2 Chic

By Design, including a party dress that's *way* too cool to lounge in the closet."

"But why this carnival?"

"A ticket to a gala event as big as I have in mind would cost a student around fifty dollars apiece." Libby shrugged and smiled brightly. "I thought that was a bit much right here at the holidays. So I came up with the idea for the carnival. Pretty cool, huh?"

Bob Gordon smiled and nodded into the camera. "Pretty cool, Libby, and generous, too. How is the carnival going?"

"Just great," Libby said. "It's done as well as you can expect. As long as you're not expecting Ringling Brothers or Barnum and Bailey. You've got to keep in mind we're working with a lot of amateurs here. But we've tried really hard."

"We?" Sabrina broke through the crowd, not believing what she was hearing. "There was no 'we.' You weren't here, Libby! You haven't been here a single night!"

"Are you getting this?" Bob Gordon asked the cameraman. The cameraman nodded. "Great! This is going to be exactly the kind of material the new show needs."

"Of course I haven't been here," Libby retorted. "If I hadn't been out with Bob Gordon soliciting local advertisers, the Harvest Moon Dance would never happen!"

"You weren't here," Sabrina said in a restrained voice. "You haven't helped with the carnival at all."

Libby nodded sadly. "That's because I knew you people were doing your best here." She turned to the crowd and held her hands out to take them all in. "Unfortunately, your best wasn't going to be good enough."

"You don't know that!"

Libby fixed her with a stare, and Sabrina could see the gleeful vindictive lights within the other girl's eyes. "As of six o'clock today, your presale of carnival tickets has been less than fifteen percent of the projected cost run of the Harvest Moon Dance. Do you honestly think that the other eighty-five percent will be reached during the carnival tomorrow night?"

"Maybe," Sabrina said uncertainly.

"See?" Libby said to the camera's audience. "That's what I admire about Sabrina: her pluckiness. Courageous in the face of adversity. But you have to know your limits."

"How dare you say that!" Sabrina exclaimed. Her comment drew a chorus of support from the volunteers. "You haven't been here helping build any of these booths. You haven't tried to sell any of the tickets."

"No," Libby agreed. "I've been working with Bob and Channel Eight to save the Harvest Moon Dance."

"How?" Sabrina challenged.

"Bob and I have put together a program that's going to be aired on Channel Eight on Saturday nights right before the horror movie. It's going to feature Westbridge High School. 2 Chic By Design has agreed to put up the development costs, and other local merchants are going to buy advertising time on the show."

Sabrina couldn't believe her ears.

"That's right," Libby said gleefully, "it's not just going to be a dance anymore, it's going to be a weekly television show!"

There was a moment of stunned silence, then the volunteers in the gym let out a ragged cheer. Sabrina could only stand there and watch as Libby basked in her latest triumph.

"Okay," Bob Gordon said after a time, "I think we've got enough footage here. Kill the camera."

The cameraman put the camcorder away.

"Come on, Libby," Bob Gordon said, "let's get out of here and to a restaurant. My treat."

"Sure, Bob," Libby replied. "I'll be right with you." She turned to Sabrina and spoke low enough so no one could overhear. "Say goodbye to the Harvest Moon Dance, Sabrina, because now it's mine!"

"You can't do this, Libby."

"Can't do what? Swipe the dance out of your hands? It's already been done, loser. And I'm putting a ban on space creatures and star men.

Catch you later." Libby turned and walked away.

Sabrina collapsed on a stack of plywood in the gym, feeling dulled and empty after Libby's exit.

Harvey stood at her side and looked confused. "A couple of days ago you said if Libby had gotten involved in the dance, things would have been better. If she's got a sponsor for the dance, isn't that a good thing?"

Sabrina glanced around the gym. A handful of the night's volunteers had followed with Libby's group, wanting to be part of the action with the Channel Eight telecast. The rest of them had slowed down work considerably, talking about everything that had just happened. "Libby did that by leading everyone to believe that we *haven't* got it together."

Harvey shook his head. "I didn't hear it that way. Libby kept talking about how hard we were trying to get it together."

Sabrina felt her frustration building at Harvey and knew that it was definitely in the wrong place. Harvey just had a big heart and couldn't really bring himself to believe bad things about people. When it came to Libby, he didn't have a clue.

Only a few hammers rose and fell in the gym because most of the volunteers were busy talking to each other. "And if we don't want the carnival to be a total bust," Harvey went on, "we'd better get back to work."

"You're right," Sabrina replied. "Maybe not about the Libby thing, but about the work thing." *And it would do me good to hit something with a hammer and work out the aggression I'm feeling.*

"Hey, look," someone called out a few minutes later. "Parents!"

Sabrina glanced up from the piles of dunking-tank parts surrounding her. The instructions were spread across her knees, and she was trying to make sense of them.

"Aren't those your aunts, Sabrina?" Valerie asked from her position beside another pile of parts.

Sure enough, Sabrina recognized Hilda and Zelda Spellman at the front of the small group of parents who had entered the gym. Dressed as they were, she almost didn't know them. After pushing herself up, Sabrina walked over to her aunts. "What are you doing here?"

Zelda wore a tapered charcoal-gray coverall and a carpenter's tool belt around her slim hips. "We came to help, of course. Hilda and I took it onto ourselves to start our own recruitment drive among the parents. You'd be surprised how many were willing to help out." She waved back at the twenty or more parents who filed into the gym, carrying tools and snack items.

"How did you get their phone numbers?" Sabrina asked.

Hilda, wearing a denim coverall with plastic protective glasses hanging around her neck and holding a protective helmet under one arm, smiled at Sabrina and said in her thickest fake German accent, "Ve haff our vays, Ms. Spellman. In de end, dey all break." She triggered the pistol-shaped battery-powered screwdriver in her hand.

"From the list of numbers you had on the home computer," Zelda answered. "Many of the other parents had prior commitments tonight, but many of them were like us and were waiting for an invitation from you. I hope you don't mind."

"Not tonight," Sabrina answered tiredly. "Tonight, I'm really glad to see you."

"Well," Zelda said, raising her eyebrows, "I guess that will have to stand for unbridled enthusiasm."

With the parents, many of whom had worked on projects around their houses and had tools of their own, the carnival was finished by eleven-fifteen that night. Although the carnival was built, the pizza was demolished, and a good time was had by all.

Sabrina filled her aunts in on what she knew about Libby's latest scheme on the way home. But even the anger she felt didn't keep her eyes open. She was asleep when they reached the house. She made a valiant effort at getting out and walking up to her room, then gave up and zapped herself to bed.

"Sabrina, wake up."

Struggling to rouse herself, Sabrina cracked one groggy eyelid and scanned her immediate vicinity for the alarm clock. Then she noticed she was twisted up in the sheets and blankets nearly four feet above her bed. She dropped at once, luckily landing near the middle of the bed.

"Sabrina, are you awake?" It was Aunt Hilda, calling from the other side of her bedroom door.

"I'm awake, I'm awake." Sabrina peered at the clock and discovered the time was 7:41 A.M.

"That's good," Hilda said, barging into the room.

A familiar tingle filled Sabrina, letting her know she'd been zapped. Her pillow disappeared from her hands. When she opened her eyes, she found herself on the living room couch downstairs. "Aunt Hilda!" she groaned.

Hilda popped into place beside her, then pointed herself up a cup of coffee. "I knew you'd want to see this. Channel Eight is breaking the story on Libby Chessler in a few minutes."

"I can wait on bad news," Sabrina replied.

"They also showed some footage about the carnival," Zelda put in from the rocker across the room.

"Did you happen to remember that I have a television in my room?" Sabrina asked testily. "And did you consider the fact that a VCR could record the news broadcast so I could see it later?" Still, her eyes were glued to the television screen. Watching Libby in full destruct mode was mesmerizing.

"Yes," Zelda said, "and we decided that we wanted to be here for you if it's too bad."

The morning weekend news anchor introduced the story, letting viewers know that Bob Gordon had produced the special feature. The camera cut away to a live piece showing Bob Gordon sitting in a chair on an interview set. "Many parents and adults today talk about teenagers as having no sense of responsibility, as being part of the the-world-owes-me crowd. This week I found the following story about a group of teens at Westbridge High who are working at being self-sufficient."

"Hey, now this isn't so bad," Sabrina said, getting more comfortable on the couch.

"That's what Napoléon's soldiers were saying when they invaded Russia," Salem replied from the back of the couch. "Then the Russian winter set in. Boy, did they change their tunes."

"Students at Westbridge High," Bob Gordon said, "wanted a school dance before the major holidays are upon us. Instead of asking the school or their parents to donate the necessary funding to implement that dream, they took it upon themselves to reach that goal. So they came up with the idea for a carnival, which will be held at Westbridge tonight."

"Now that sounds like good advertising," Hilda said.

Sabrina was thinking the same thing.

The view on the television changed, playing some of the footage of the work on the carnival that had been shot last night. Watching it was agony to Sabrina. Nothing looked ready. All the bright colors of the booths looked artificial, as effective as Band-Aids that had been placed over huge zits in hopes of disguising them.

"It looked much more promising than this when we left it last night," Zelda offered.

Sabrina couldn't say anything. The aroma coming off the hot chocolate in her hands didn't even smell appetizing anymore. She pointed it away. "But this is what people who see this story are going to think it looks like."

"All week long," Bob Gordon said on television, "a group of Westbridge High students have labored diligently to make this carnival a success. But according to this reporter's sources, less than fifteen percent of the necessary tickets to fund the school dance have been sold."

More footage rolled of the carnival, making it look like a cast-off attempt that a group of kindergartners had put together. Sabrina grew more and more mortified. She could just imagine the ticket sales nuking down.

"However," Bob Gordon continued, "adversity has a way of bringing on champions, men and women who rise above the struggle to become heroes. And that's the story I'm bringing to you this morning. I'd like to introduce the heroine of the Westbridge Harvest Moon Dance effort: Miss Libby Chessler."

The camera drew back, drawing tight on Libby. She looked as radiant as ever, dressed in a 2 Chic By Design business skirt and blouse. Her hair was pulled back, giving her a trendy professional look.

Sabrina couldn't believe it. *The heroine of the Westbridge Harvest Moon Dance?* She wanted to scream.

Chapter 4

"Good morning, Libby," Bob Gordon said on
the television set in the Spellman home as Sabrina sat frozen and staring at the screen. "I'm glad
you could join us at such an early hour. Especially after the late hours you put in working on
the carnival last night."

"Thank you for having me, Bob," Libby said
with saccharine sweetness. "I'm glad to be here."

Maybe you shouldn't be so glad to be there,
Sabrina thought. She brought her hand up, carefully extending her forefinger toward the television screen.

"No," Zelda said.

"Don't even think about it," Hilda added.

Sabrina curled her finger back to neutral.
"Well, it's too late not to think about it."

"Aw, c'mon!" Salem said. "It'll only be one

tiny zap. Over before you know it, and nobody will be the wiser."

"No," Zelda repeated. "The last thing you'd want is for mention of something like this to get back to the Witches' Council. And breaking Federal Communications Commission rulings about using witchcraft over an open broadcast signal would bring about dire consequences as well."

"Drell had a big part in setting up the FCC regulations," Hilda said proudly. "Ever since that Orson Welles *War of the Worlds* scare, the Witches' Council has had to acknowledge the threat of radio and television."

"Tell me," Bob Gordon said to Libby, "did you ever think the Harvest Moon Dance would take place?"

"You saw the carnival, Bob. Until I was able to secure another means to fund the dance, we were really struggling."

"Tell us what happened."

"I suppose most of the people out there have recognized me as the 2 Chic By Design model from Saturday nights," Libby said with a smile.

"The commercials you've done for the 2 Chic By Design boutique have drawn a lot of local attention."

"The advertising people seem to be really happy with me," Libby stated. "Happy enough that when I went to them with the idea of doing a television show about the students of Westbridge High, they immediately said yes."

"A television show?" Sabrina repeated.

"That's right," Bob Gordon said proudly. "Libby Chessler is going to be the hostess of a brand-new, real-situation program airing here on Channel Eight on Saturday nights before the horror movie. Tell us about the show."

"Well, first of all it's going to be called *Real Life High,*" Libby said. "It's going to be about growth and development. Interpersonal relationships. You'll see intense emotion and kids dealing with today's issues. We're not going to be working from a script. We're going to be working from events that actually happen to the student body of Westbridge High."

"It sounds interesting," Bob Gordon commented.

"Oh, it will be," Libby promised. "In fact, we have a clip of one of those events."

Even though she thought she'd been astonished before, Sabrina wasn't at all prepared for what came next. Before her eyes, the television set blinked, then rolled the footage again from the carnival. The first clip was of Libby as she drove nails on one of the booths. The camera perspective changed again, showing another scene from the carnival. Sabrina saw herself, her face red with emotion, her hair in disarray from working all afternoon, squaring off against

48

Libby. But the film was edited till it looked as if Sabrina was venting at Libby, totally attacking her.

"There was no 'we,'" the television Sabrina said. "You weren't here, Libby! You haven't been here a single night! You haven't helped with the carnival at all. You haven't been here helping build any of these booths. You haven't tried to sell any of the tickets."

"That was all the truth," Sabrina said in a stunned voice as the television view went back to the set with Bob Gordon and Libby.

"That must have been hard to take," Bob Gordon told Libby gently.

"Oh, it was," Libby replied in a halting voice. "I'd always thought of Sabrina as such a friend, but she's secretly been resentful of my successes."

"Evidently quite resentful," Bob Gordon said.

"Those are the kinds of stories *Real Life High* is going to be focusing on," Libby said. "They'll be filled with the real world of Westbridge High."

"Sounds fab, to use an idiom of the jargon viewers will probably find on an episode of your new show."

Libby just smiled. "The coolest thing is that 2 Chic By Design is going to totally fund the Harvest Moon Dance for Westbridge. So in three weeks the audience will have the chance to go to the dance with us."

"We'll be looking forward to it," Bob Gordon said, turning toward the camera. "And remember, *Real Life High* debuts this Saturday night, right here on Channel Eight."

Knowing the camera was about to cut back to the news program's main anchor and unable to restrain herself any longer, Sabrina pointed at the television set. *Let's see how your new television image handles a sudden burst of static electricity,* she thought at Libby. *When your hair finishes standing up on end, the only modeling you'll be able to get will be as a poster child for the follically impaired!*

"Sabrina!" Zelda exclaimed, gesturing at almost the same instant as Sabrina.

A bright flurry of rainbow-colored sparkles smashed into the console television, rocking it back as if it had been captured in the throes of an earthquake. The sparkles surrounded the television, fizzling out in rapid succession. Before the last spark expired, though, the television fell into what looked like a million tiny pieces.

"Ooops!" Sabrina cried out. "Sorry!"

"Sorry?" Zelda asked. "Do you realize what you almost did?"

Almost? The sudden realization that her aunt had managed to stop her spell sank into Sabrina and brought a feeling of instant relief. And remorse. After what she'd done, Libby really did deserve to get zapped.

"Yes," she replied.

Zelda looked stern; then that look softened. "I'm as angry as you are, sweetheart, but you can't just go throwing your powers around like that."

"Do you know how much Libby hurt the carnival just now?" Sabrina asked.

"We don't know that yet," Zelda said calmly. "After all, any publicity is supposed to be good publicity. Even bad publicity."

"I guess we'll have to wait and see, won't we?"

"Yes."

Still angry and put off, Sabrina raised her hand, ready to zap herself up to her room. "Then I hope you don't mind if I wait in my room."

"As a matter of fact, I do mind."

Sabrina's heart sank. *Punishment. Why does there always have to be punishment afterward?*

"You're going to put that television back together." Zelda rose from the rocking chair and walked to the kitchen.

Glumly Sabrina pointed at the pile of pieces on the floor. But her finger didn't work.

"You'll have to do it the old-fashioned way," Zelda said. "Your magic won't work."

"But I'm not a television repairman."

Zelda glanced back at her. "You'll find upon

closer inspection of those pieces that you don't have to be."

Moving from the couch, Sabrina peered down at the jumbled television pieces. Expecting to find bits and pieces of metal and plastics, she was really surprised to find—

"Jigsaw puzzle pieces?" Sabrina picked up a handful of pieces, confirming what they were.

"That's right. Three hundred of them to be exact."

"I have to put puzzle pieces together to fix the television?"

"Unless you'd prefer Legos."

Sabrina's protest froze when she realized her aunt meant it.

"Legos are a three-dimensional medium," Hilda whispered as she got up from the couch and went to join her sister in the kitchen. "Stick with the puzzle pieces."

"Okay." Sabrina sighed. "The puzzle will be enough."

"I hope so," Zelda replied. "It will give you time to think about things. Libby may be a pain right now, Sabrina, but dealing with her with your witchcraft is out of the question. Don't give up on yourself or your dreams."

Looking at the pile of puzzle pieces, Sabrina thought maybe giving up wasn't such a bad idea. Except there was a piece of her that refused to

knuckle under to Libby. There had to
Didn't there?

"Sabrina," Zelda called from the kitchen after
answering the phone.

"Yes?" Sabrina had to push her way back out
from under the coffee table. She'd found 299
pieces of the 300-piece puzzle in the last two and
a half hours. Piecing it together had been a pain,
but it had given her a lot of time to think things
through. Unfortunately, though her anger had
mostly gone, no plans had come to mind concerning what to do with Libby.

"Harvey's on the phone."

"I'll take it in here." Rocking back, she
pointed up a wireless extension on the coffee
table, then answered it. Pointing one up saved on
the hassle of trying to find the wireless each time.
"Harvey, hi."

Zelda hung up the other phone with a click.

"Hey, Sab, thought I'd call and make sure it
was cool to come on over." There was just a hint
of sleepiness that remained in Harvey's voice,
making him sound incredibly cute.

"Sure, it's fine." Frantically Sabrina reached
under the couch again, flailing away with one
hand to find the missing puzzle piece. Where
could it have gone? All the other pieces had been
nearby.

"Will you be ready in about twenty minutes?
If we hurry we can still make breakfast."

"Sounds great." Sabrina pointed at all the furniture and levitated it over the floor. She scanned under each piece, finding no sign of the missing puzzle piece.

"Sabrina!" Hilda called out. "What do you think you're doing?"

Startled, Sabrina let the furniture drop to the floor with a chorus of thumps.

"What happened?" Harvey asked.

"I dropped something," Sabrina answered. "It's okay." Promising to be ready on time, she got Harvey off the phone.

"What's wrong?" Hilda asked, pointing the pieces of furniture back into their proper places.

"I'm missing one of the puzzle pieces," Sabrina complained, looking at the nearly finished puzzle. It was of the console television, complete with a picture of Libby and Bob Gordon frozen on it.

"Are you sure?"

Sabrina pointed at Bob Gordon's missing left eyebrow. "I'm sure."

"And it's nowhere on the floor?"

"I haven't found it yet, and I've been all over this floor for the last ten minutes."

"Ahem."

On her hands and knees, very aware of the clock ticking off the seconds, Sabrina glanced up at Salem, who sat in the doorway of the kitchen with his tail curled around himself. "What?" she asked.

54

"I could help you," the cat suggested.

"I thought you had a breakfast to attend to," Sabrina said sarcastically.

"I did. Hours ago."

"Then isn't lunch in there somewhere? Or maybe a brunch, then you can still do lunch."

"I'm trying to work up my appetite."

"Do you know where the piece is?" Sabrina asked suspiciously.

"I could help you look," Salem answered.

Sabrina glared at the cat, remembering how he'd come by to inspect the pile of puzzle pieces earlier. "Did you *take* one of those pieces, Salem?"

"Me?" The cat struggled to look innocent.

Sabrina saw through the effort immediately. "You did!"

"I want to offer you a deal," Salem said.

"If I'm late for this date," Sabrina promised, "you're going to need to join the Witches' Protection Program to be safe again."

"Suppose I find that missing piece," Salem said, "thereby freeing you from your punishment? Would you be willing to let me go to the carnival tonight?"

"No."

"Are you sure?" Salem uncurled his tail from his front paws and swirled it around the floor in front of him. "I mean, you might want to give your answer a little more thought."

"No," Sabrina answered. "Give me the missing puzzle piece." She held out her hand.

"I haven't found it yet." Salem turned his head away. "But I'm looking even though I seem to have lost my enthusiasm for the hunt."

"I'm being blackmailed by my own cat?" Sabrina asked.

"Blackmail is such an ugly word, don't you think?"

"Salem."

"Yes?" The cat licked his lips and looked at her expectantly.

"Maybe I can't fix the television without that puzzle piece you've hidden, but I can do this." Sabrina pointed at the nearby rubber mouse toy.

The rubber mouse grew to twice the size of the cat and became animated. It stretched its rubbery legs out and advanced on Salem, ears flattening against its head.

"Okay, okay!" Salem flicked the puzzle piece out from under his paw, sending it skidding across the floor.

Sabrina captured the piece and put it into the puzzle. Immediately the television reformed, thankfully in the middle of some cartoon instead of *The Bob Gordon and Libby Chessler Mutual Admiration Show.*

"TV's all done," she called out to Zelda.

"Thank you," her aunt replied. "Remember, Hilda and I will be at the carnival tonight, so no witchcraft."

"I know." Sabrina zapped the toy mouse back down to its original size and state of inactivity, then zapped herself to her room. She still wasn't happy. Without witchcraft, how was she going to handle Libby and all the damage Libby had done to the carnival?

Harvey seemed uncomfortable at breakfast. He and Sabrina shared a back booth in the fast-food restaurant that they'd shared before on other weekend mornings. A tiny spell Sabrina had learned from her magical handbook kept the booth always available anytime they came in. Small children had already filled up the indoor play area, and harried adults rushed in, vainly hoping to make up lost time.

"Something's on your mind, Harvey," she said, when she couldn't ignore it any longer.

"Yeah, I guess there is. You heard about the television show Libby's going to be doing at Channel Eight?"

"I might have heard something about it."

"She called me this morning," Harvey said, "and asked me to be on her show."

"Gee," Sabrina forced herself to say, keeping her smile in place, "you must be really excited." Without warning, a sudden peal of thunder gusted outside. Knowing her emotions had disturbed the atmosphere, Sabrina worked hard to keep herself under control.

"Wow." Harvey looked out the window. "I

heard on the weather that it was supposed to rain tonight, but that came like out of nowhere."

"Meteorology, way beyond anything I'm doing these days. But I'm sure there's an explanation. So what did you tell Libby?"

"Nothing," Harvey replied. "I wanted to talk to you first."

At first Sabrina was happy. Then the realization that Harvey could have said no without her dawned slowly. What he needed help with was saying *yes*. "You want to do this?" she asked.

Harvey looked away again, then grinned sheepishly. "Sounds kind of lame, doesn't it? Me thinking I'd be good enough to be on a television show. I mean, what would I do?"

"Harvey," Sabrina said, "I think you'd be great on television."

"Then it's okay if I tell Libby yes?"

"Sure." *I want you to do everything you want to, Harvey Kinkle, but sometimes what you want to do scares me. Like now.*

"I'm glad you don't mind," he told her.

I didn't say that.

"Libby's called a meeting this afternoon," Harvey went on. "An organizational get-together, she called it. I know I'm supposed to be at the carnival early this afternoon to help finish setting up, but—"

"Go ahead and go to the meeting," Sabrina encouraged, though it was the last thing she wanted to do. "We'll have plenty of help there.

And my aunts and some of the parents from last night will be there as well."

Sabrina stepped out of one of the dressing stalls in the girls' locker room in the gym. She checked her outfit, wondering if there was anything else she could do to it.

"You're a clown!" Valerie gasped when she saw her in the mirror.

"You noticed," Sabrina said. "And I thought I hid it so well."

Valerie whirled around, taking in the baggy pants, big shoes, really wide tie, and the Day-Glo orange hair. *"Why* are you a clown? You're supposed to be a hostess."

"Because suddenly there's a shortage of clowns," Sabrina answered, feeling depressed. "And we promised clowns at the carnival."

"We have no clowns?" Dressed in a clingy green dress with darker green sequins, Valerie looked dynamic.

Sabrina held up a hand with four fingers extended. All those fingers were encased in a bright red glove. "There are four of us now. Only three other people decided they still wanted to be clowns after they learned about Libby's television show. Everybody believes that Libby's going to show up here tonight, and they don't want their faces covered by greasepaint if they get the chance to be on television."

"Oh, Sabrina," Valerie said sympathetically.

59

"I saw that dress you were going to wear. It was beautiful."

"It still is," Sabrina said. "There'll be another time to wear it." *I hope.* She slapped at the enormous stomach the clown suit's underwiring created, making the whole thing wobble dramatically. "But tonight it's big shoes and a red rubber nose for me."

Valerie appeared hesitant, then asked, "Is there another clown suit?"

Sabrina pointed at the boxes sitting beside the row of lockers. "Plenty."

"Think the carnival has room for one more clown?"

"You? You don't have to do that."

"If you can do it, then I can, too. I insist. After all, we did promise clowns." Valerie walked back to the costume boxes and started going through them. "I'm just glad the acrobats seem to be interested in doing their act. Rolling around on the floor sounds really tiring and painful." She took the clown suit back to a stall and started getting dressed.

Sabrina walked to the mirror and looked at herself. Only her face still looked like Sabrina. And she was about to change that. She took out the makeup case that came with the clown costume and wondered where to begin. No matter which color she chose, though, none of them looked right. And exactly in what order did the makeup go on?

*"Mirror on the wall, don't let me down,
Guide my hand, give me the face of a clown."*

Then she pointed at the mirror. Her hands tingled, then took on a life of their own, showing no hesitation at all as they painted her face.

When they'd finished, a sad-faced clown with bright blue teardrops on her cheeks was reflected in the mirror. With bright Day-Glo orange hair, of course.

"Hey, that's really cool," Valerie said as she emerged in her own clown suit. Her wig was a bright Day-Glo green. "Can you do my face?"

"Sure," Sabrina said. The magic spell still filled her hands. In just a few minutes she expertly rendered Valerie's face into that of a clown with a goofy smile.

Valerie stood at her side as they looked into the mirror, sad face and goofy face. Despite the fact that she hadn't wanted to dress as a clown, Sabrina thought the effort looked really good. *Maybe being a clown won't be so bad,* she thought.

"Now this is a Kodak moment!" Valerie exclaimed.

A trio of girls entered the locker room, all of them looking terrific in their outfits. Sabrina recognized them from her classes and from seeing them in the hallways.

"Omigosh!" one of them screamed dramatically. "Someone's sent in the clowns!" Together, all three girls cowered against the wall, then burst out laughing.

"Or not," Sabrina said, leading the way out of the locker room. Could things get any more miserable?

Chapter 5

Twenty-five minutes before the carnival was officially slated to open, the rainstorm the weather teams across the local channels and radio stations had been promising cut loose with electrifying fury.

Sabrina stood in the foyer outside the gym and watched the rain come pelting down. For added enjoyment pea-size hail rattled the windows threateningly. And there was the seemingly ever-present jagged lightning.

Valerie joined Sabrina at the window, and they gazed up at the leaden gray sky. "Maybe you should have put sad faces on both of us," Valerie suggested.

"I know."

"A few people have shown up for the carnival."

"I saw them." Maybe as many as two dozen people had shown up for the carnival early, but Sabrina knew that was probably because the parents had promised their kids to bring them and planned to come early and leave early. All of which meant low ticket sales.

"Jeremy's doing a good job in there," Valerie said.

Sabrina nodded. "I watched him. He's a good fortune-teller." And Jeremy was. He had a knack for drawing in whoever wanted his fortune told.

"Loved the costume you came up with for him," Valerie said, talking about the long black robe covered in sigils and zodiac signs, and the dark purple swami turban sprouting midnight blue peacock feathers.

"Oh, that," Sabrina said. "That was nothing. Just something I found lying around the house."

Thunder pealed suddenly, shaking the glass in the windows, and a fresh wave of rain spilled from the dark sky.

"Where's Harvey?" Valerie asked. "I thought he'd be here by now."

"So did I," Sabrina admitted. Even as much as she trusted Harvey, she was beginning to wonder what was going on. Was he going to stand her and the carnival up to be on Libby's show?

* * *

"Hey, Sab, sorry I'm late."

Sabrina turned to Harvey, feeling angry at him because it was almost fifteen minutes after seven and they were swamped. Literally. Evidently the inclement weather hadn't deterred most of the Westbridge parents and teens who'd bought tickets to the carnival.

But although she wanted to be angry with Harvey, she couldn't help but feel sorry for him. He was thoroughly drenched from the rainstorm. "How did you get so soaked?" she asked, grabbing a nearby towel and mopping at him with it.

"I didn't want to take any of the close parking places," Harvey answered. "So I parked really far back."

Sabrina worked a spell into the towel she was using, causing it to dry much more thoroughly than it normally would. She hoped Harvey wouldn't notice. "With the weather and all, I was getting worried about you."

"It was Libby's organizational meeting," Harvey said. "I was going to leave, but Mr. Gordon asked me to stay a little longer because he and Libby thought I might have a lot of what he called high-profile points."

"I see." *And I'll just bet I know who gave Bob Gordon that opinion,* Sabrina thought. "So the meeting's over?" It would be nice to know when to expect Libby.

"No," Harvey said, taking the towel from her

hands. "I left when nobody was watching. So am I forgiven?"

"Yes. You worked so hard to help put the carnival together, what's being a few minutes late?"

Harvey shivered. "So what's up with the clown costume? I thought you were dressing up as something else."

"We had a shortage of clowns." Sabrina suddenly remembered how she was dressed and felt totally uncool. The big belly of the clown suit might be funny looking, but it possessed less than zero in attraction.

"You look really great as a clown, Sab."

"I do?"

"Yeah. Those feet are enormous." Harvey grinned. "It must be really cool goofing with the little kids."

"The ones that enjoy clowns," Sabrina said. "But to some of them, a clown is just a target."

"You said you didn't have enough clowns. Does that mean you have an extra costume that will fit me?"

"They're pretty much one size fits all," Sabrina answered.

"Then I'll be a clown. At least I'll get some dry clothes out of the deal."

"You're supposed to be helping run the football toss," Sabrina pointed out. "A clown might not be appreciated there."

"Sab, let's think about this. It's one thing for

Harvey Kinkle to taunt the guys out there wanting to impress the girls, but can you imagine what it's going to be like for them to get heckled by a guy in a red rubber nose?"

Harvey's prediction proved true. Putting a clown behind the counter at the football toss beefed up the ticket purchases there.

Sabrina left him there, getting back to working the crowd that had steadily grown since seven o'clock. While Valerie and the other clowns passed out helium balloons and suckers, Sabrina performed small magic tricks. Of course, they looked like sleight-of-hand, but she actually used real magic to pluck suckers out of thin air and plastic flowers out of her voluminous sleeves.

Westbridge community continued to turn out in staggering numbers to the Westbridge High carnival. And one of the biggest hits was Jeremy's fortune-telling.

"Who's the young man in Uncle Tobias's old robe?"

Sabrina turned around and found her aunt Zelda standing behind her. Zelda was dressed as a ringmaster, complete with a top hat and tails. A coiled whip hung beside one jodhpur-clad hip.

"His name is Jeremy Hiller," Sabrina answered. "I hope you don't mind me borrowing the robe."

"Not at all. It's hung down in the dungeon for decades. I think Tobias would be flattered if he could see it put to use at this carnival. Jeremy's good."

"How's Hilda doing?"

"You're going to be giving away more prizes at the Weight and Age Guess booth than you'd originally planned. The carnival-goers have learned Hilda's weak spot."

"What?"

"Weight." Zelda led the way over to the booth.

"Weight isn't that hard to guess within five or ten pounds," Sabrina said.

Hilda stood to one side of a scale. She wore long flowing powder-blue robes that looked faintly Eastern in origin, and a metal headband set with a feathered serpent at the center above her eyebrows.

A girl stepped in front of Hilda and waited. Sabrina recognized her from a class they'd shared last semester. Her name was Beth.

Hilda made a show of examining the girl, then announced, "Ninety-five pounds."

"No way!" Sabrina exclaimed. It was easy to see that, although Beth wasn't fat, she weighed around one hundred ten to one hundred twenty pounds.

Beth stepped onto the scales.

Hilda peered at the scale, then shook her head. She reached up to the wall behind her and took down a brightly colored stuffed toucan. Beth walked away with her prize.

"You see," Zelda said, folding her arms, "it's hard for Hilda to guess the weight of other people when she *knows* she's a perfect one hundred ten pounds herself."

Sabrina groaned when she looked at the long line that had formed in front of Hilda's booth. The line there was almost as long as the one in front of Jeremy Hiller's booth. "Do we have plenty of prizes?"

"Hilda zaps up a fresh basket of stuffed animals whenever she needs to. I relieved the girl who was helping her to hand out the prizes myself. That way no one knows we've run out twice already."

"At least everybody's going to go away happy."

"I'd better go hand out more stuffed animals," Zelda said. "Hilda's sped up her guessing."

"If you need anything, let me know."

Zelda smiled as Hilda gave away a stuffed chimpanzee. "The good thing is that there are a lot of people here tonight."

"I know. I just hope it's enough to fund the dance."

Libby arrived at eight-thirty, with a full entourage of her hangers-on and a Channel Eight film crew right behind her. The carnival audience took notice of her at once, and in no time at all the crowd around Libby swelled dramatically.

Fortunately, Libby was partially trapped by her fame. The crowd held her in place, preventing her from going to the carnival attractions. At the same time, though, things started to go wrong.

The food court temporarily lost power due to a lightning flash. Sabrina and Valerie checked the power supply and found that the breaker had been damaged in the power surge. While Valerie went to check with one of the parents who'd worked as an electrician, Sabrina zapped the breaker into working order again.

The parent checked the breaker and declared it was fine. The food service continued on, mostly uninterrupted.

Then the dunking tank sprang a leak, which caused a minor commotion. Harvey and some of the other boys managed to pull the liner around, with a little magical assist from Sabrina, and got the leak to seal. The dunking tank was only down a few minutes after a mop and bucket brigade was organized.

But Coach Taylor, Westbridge's basketball coach, nearly went apoplectic. He was on hand to oversee the carnival and made a spectacle of himself by insisting on taking charge of the mopping. Luckily, Zelda freed Hilda from the weight guessing booth, and Hilda was able to distract the basketball coach with her charms.

Unfortunately, her attention to the coach triggered an attack of jealousy on the part of Vice-principal Kraft. To her credit, Hilda proved capable of handling both men.

In that time, though, Libby and the news crew picked up momentum.

And everybody wanted Sabrina's attention because the crowd in the gym suddenly grew so large it got out of hand. A group of boys standing in line started pushing one another in play, then ended up accidentally knocking loose one of the support cables for the tent materials over the booths.

Designed to help tear down the carnival quickly, the cable was responsible for allowing the tents to collapse prematurely. In seconds all of the booths were covered by yards of fat, blobby multicolored mushroom-shaped cloth.

Libby made sure the film crew didn't miss the photo opportunity. While Sabrina was helping pull the cable tight to raise the cloth off the booths, she lost track of Libby.

Taking a brief respite while more help was summoned, Sabrina ducked outside the gym and into the janitor's closet they had access to. Inside, she zapped herself back to the Spellman house.

Salem lay stretched out on the arm of the couch, idly batting the rubber mouse high into the air, then batting it up again when it came back down. "He's got a real hot streak going, folks. Look at that style, look at that form, look at that cat go!" He batted the rubber mouse, sending it spinning into the air again.

"Salem," Sabrina called.

"Yeow!" Salem squealed when he looked at her. He flipped over and bounded to his feet as he took cover behind one of the couch's throw pillows. "Sabrina, what do you think you're doing sneaking up on me? Don't you know you could scare me out of a life or three?"

"Look," Sabrina said, knowing she had to get back to the carnival as soon as possible, "do you still want to go to the carnival?"

Salem stepped from behind the throw pillow. "And what is this all about? You've suddenly decided you're my fairy godclown?"

"I need someone to spy on Libby," Sabrina answered.

"Moi?"

"Libby knows Hilda and Zelda."

"So I was chosen by default?"

"Are you coming or not?"

"I don't want to appear too eager. So what do I do?"

"Keep an eye on Libby and let me know what she's up to," Sabrina said.

"That sounds like a lot of running."

"Not with these." Sabrina pointed at Salem,

then at her own wrist. Instantly thick black watches appeared on both of them.

Salem glanced at the one that had settled just above his paw. "Dick Crazy wristwatches?"

"They're not just wristwatches," Sabrina told the cat. "They're two-way wristradios. We can keep in touch this way."

"This is kind of bulky," Salem complained. "Why didn't you point up some of those nifty little headsets like Tom Cruise used in *Mission: Impossible?*"

"A headset on a cat would be really conspicuous, don't you think?"

Salem held up the leg with the Dick Crazy two-way wristradio. "And this is better?"

"Salem!"

"All right, all right! Let's go."

Sabrina zapped them both back to the carnival.

Two off-duty police officers who'd agreed to work security for the carnival got the rescue effort organized to save the booths. They used a device one of them called a come-along to leverage the cable back into place. But the work went slowly because the tension on the cable was heavy and the helpful police officers were afraid of breaking it.

Sabrina and Valerie redoubled their efforts as clowns, trying to keep the crowd from getting disgruntled and demanding their money back while the booths were being fixed.

"Sabrina, our target's on the move again," Salem called over the Dick Crazy wristradio.

"Okay," Sabrina said, handing out suckers to every kid she could find. She'd last seen Libby filming some commentary in front of the fallen tent material.

"She's turned the corner and is proceeding to the football toss," Salem went on.

Harvey! Sabrina thought, knowing Libby would use her television show to influence Harvey. *Wonder how she'll like him as a clown?*

Slowly the tent booths rose. But the damage was already done. It had taken almost thirty minutes to get the booths operational again. They'd lost part of the crowd.

"We had to return money for some of the tickets," Valerie said. "Parents got worn out waiting with their kids for the booths to reopen."

"Our target has set her sights, Control," Salem said over the wristradio. "She—"

Sabrina clapped her hand over the Dick Crazy wristradio, shutting off the transmission.

Valerie looked confused. "What's wrong with your watch?"

"It's not my watch," Sabrina explained. "It's a joke watch. See?" She held it up so Valerie could see the writing on the side. "Dick Crazy, like the comic strip."

"Didn't Warren Beatty play him in a movie?"

"That was another character," Sabrina said. "Look, there's nothing we can do about the refunds."

"I know. I just thought you'd want to know."

"I do. I'm glad you told me, but 'et's keep things moving here for the attendees we have left."

"Right." Valerie wandered off, handing out more helium balloons. Basically, though, she was giving them to kids who already had them.

Sabrina uncovered the wristradio and found Salem in the midst of another surveillance update.

"And is on her way to the fortune-teller's booth," the cat reported. "Hey! Isn't that Uncle Tobias's robe?"

"Never mind that," Sabrina instructed as she made her way toward Jeremy Hiller's booth.

"Oh, yeah," Salem said, "our target has vectored in on the fortune-teller's twenty."

"Enough with the spy talk."

"I was just getting into character."

"I didn't ask you for character," Sabrina said, "I just wanted periodic updates."

The line in front of the fortune-teller's booth was still long, but Libby had cut through the waiting people. She stood on the other side of the table Jeremy was using to spread out the tarot cards. The camcorder operator stood to one side of Libby so he could film her conversation with Jeremy.

"So how long have you been a fortune-teller?" Libby asked.

Jeremy's attention was completely locked on the camera lens. His mouth worked like a goldfish's, and his eyes were big and round. His complexion didn't look good, either.

"Just to-tonight," Jeremy said in a forced, hoarse whisper.

Libby knows how shy Jeremy is! Sabrina realized. *She's deliberately embarrassing him!* She tried to get through the crowd to Jeremy, but even then she didn't know how she was going to save him from Libby.

"It seems as if you've attracted a large number of people who want to hear how their future is going to go," Libby said. "Maybe you'd like to tell our audience about some of the more interesting predictions you've made tonight." She moved a handheld microphone in front of Jeremy's face.

Suddenly Jeremy shot to his feet, knocking over his chair behind him. "I'm g-g-g-going to hurl!" he gasped, putting both hands over his mouth.

To save Jeremy from total humiliation at Libby's hands, Sabrina pointed at him and put an antinausea spell on him. Jeremy still bolted through the crowd and was gone from view in seconds.

"You did that on purpose!" Sabrina accused Libby as she finally reached the girl.

"What?" Libby asked innocently.

The camcorder operator moved into position behind Libby, filming Sabrina.

"You know Jeremy doesn't like attention."

"No, I didn't." Libby was totally cool.

"You sabotaged him. You're trying to hurt the work everyone has done on this carnival."

Bob Gordon stood beside the camcorder operator, urging him to move and giving camera angle suggestions by putting his hands together and creating frames. "This is the kind of stuff we want. The pure essence of what being a teen in today's world is all about. The combativeness, the rivalry for attention and control, all the angst."

"Sabrina, everything I've done has been to promote the Harvest Moon Dance," Libby said. "That's what this carnival is all about, right?"

"No," Sabrina replied. "It was about everybody coming together to work for something they wanted."

"What *they* wanted?" Libby asked. "Or what *you* wanted? I don't think you've taken a good look at your own agenda lately."

Before Sabrina could think up a word in her defense, Libby brushed by and walked away. Channel Eight followed her, the camcorder operator getting final footage of Sabrina standing in stunned silence.

Chapter 6

☆

☆

Bad idea," Valerie said.

I should have unloaded on Libby, Sabrina thought as she guided Valerie back to the girls' locker area. *I should have told her exactly what I thought of everything she's done.*

Except that Libby might have been hoping that Sabrina would try that. Libby *had* waited for a while, maybe giving her time to do exactly that.

"I mean it," Valerie went on as she entered the locker room. "This is one of your *worst* ideas. I'm not a fortune-teller."

"Think positive," Sabrina replied. "How hard can it be? Money, romance, a nice car. And mention fulfillment a lot. That pretty much covers it all."

78

"I think not. Remember, I listened to Jeremy go through his spiel. He was good."

"You can be good." Sabrina pointed at the pile of boxes containing extra clown costumes.

"What are you doing?"

"Looking for your costume. I don't think people would be interested in having their fortunes told by a clown."

"All that are in there are clown costumes."

"And this." Sabrina held up a box marked Enchantress. The picture on the carton showed a woman dressed in a green minidress trimmed in black fur. The material was a print of several tiny palms and staring eyeballs. Sabrina remembered the design from a witches' party she'd gone to.

"That looks cool," Valerie said, taking the box.

"I thought you'd like it," Sabrina replied.

When Valerie stepped out of the dressing area in the green mini and had her hair brushed out, she looked stunning. "This is never going to work," Valerie said.

"It'll work." Sabrina led the way back to the fortune-teller booth.

A line of people milled around the area, waiting for the fortune-teller. There was no sign of Jeremy, however. Luckily, there was no sign of Libby, either.

Sabrina guided Valerie to the chair behind

the table. Jeremy had left the tarot cards behind.

"I can't work with these cards," Valerie whispered, stacking them together. "I don't know enough about them."

Sabrina briefly considered casting a spell on Valerie that would give her knowledge of the tarot cards. That would be hard to explain later. And she didn't want Valerie to steal any of Jeremy's accomplishments away with her magic.

"I'll be right back," Sabrina promised and hurried back into the locker room. As soon as she made sure she was alone, she zapped herself back to her aunts' house.

Sabrina's mind worked frantically as she searched through her bedroom. *All I need is a prop that will inspire Valerie and give her a little confidence.* But what?

Then she remembered an image she'd seen within the past week in the ancient handbook she'd been given by her father. She went to it, running her fingers across the surface and the title, *The Discovery of Magic*. She said a quick finder spell, then flipped the book open. *There!* The drawing showed a round black globe resting in someone's palm.

She said another spell, then reached into the page of the book. She pulled the black globe out, then zapped herself back to the locker room.

"What's that?" Valerie asked when she returned.

"Your crystal ball." Sabrina held it out for inspection.

Valerie looked at it doubtfully, then touched it with a forefinger. "Looks kind of dark, doesn't it?"

Sabrina turned the globe over, revealing the oval section in the bottom. As they watched, a triangular shape floated up out of the liquid core of the globe. Words became clear at once: OUTLOOK GOOD. "But it's easy to operate."

"A Magic Eight-Ball!" Valerie exclaimed in delight. "Now this is fortune-telling even *I* can do."

"I'm glad." *Now if Valerie doesn't suddenly develop cold feet everything should be okay.* "I'm going to go look for Jeremy. I'll be back to check on you." She hurried off. As she made her way through the booths looking for Jeremy, the weight at the end of her arm reminded her of the wristradio and Salem. The thought of Salem being loose at the carnival sent a chill down her back.

Stopping by the dart-throw booth, Sabrina pushed the transmit button on the Dick Crazy wristradio. "Salem, where are you?"

"Control, I'm on the job."

"Terrific. Where's Libby?"

"I lost her." Salem's voice sounded garbled.

"How could you lose her?"

"There are a lot of people here, Control. When I started dodging feet to get around the crowd, I looked up and she was gone."

"Where are you?" Sabrina asked again.

"What's that you say?" Salem asked. The transmission at his end was suddenly filled with static, and it sounded like the wristradio was banging against something metallic. "You're breaking up." More static sounded.

"Salem! *Salem!*"

The cat didn't bother to respond.

Knowing Salem as well as she did, Sabrina walked toward the food court. She found him crouched on top of the tent covering the hot-dog stand, a black-furred shadow stretched out and practically invisible. Sabrina wouldn't have seen him if it hadn't been for Salem's lightning-quick snatch of a Polish sausage from the grill below. Luckily, no one else noticed him.

Sabrina walked to the tent and locked eyes with the cat.

Salem's clean white fangs sank into the sausage; then his eyes widened as he saw Sabrina. "I'm found, I'm found!"

"How many of those have you eaten?"

"Counting this one?" Salem asked hopefully.

"Yes."

"Three, but it was because I didn't know how long I was going to be lost. I panicked."

"You're going home," Sabrina told him.

Salem closed his paws tightly over the sausage, hugging it to him. "No! I can stay and help—"

Sabrina pointed and he was gone, not even a loose hair remaining.

"Did you say something?" one of the girls working behind the counter asked, approaching Sabrina.

"Have you seen Libby Chessler?" Sabrina asked.

The girl nodded. "She left just a few minutes ago."

"You're sure?"

"Yes." The girl frowned and shook her head. "One of the guys that was supposed to be helping here left with her. Some dedication, huh?"

"Yeah." As Sabrina moved through the booths, she found other booth attendants who were just as irritated about attrition in the ranks. Libby had taken more of the workers away, promising them interviews on her show for next Saturday night, which had to be taped tonight. The carnival had become slightly understaffed again.

And the bad weather was starting to put a damper on the moods of all the carnival-goers.

Sabrina forced herself out of bed the next morning and glared at the clock. It was 10:45 A.M., and she felt as if she hadn't gotten any sleep at all. Even with the professional cleaning crew Mr. Gossman, one of the parents who owned a construction company, had provided, she'd been at the gym till two in the morning. She'd ushered her aunts home, taking responsibility for finishing the cleanup herself.

She only thought about the stairs briefly, then considered all the aches and pains that filled her body. Convinced unnecessary physical exertion was out of the question, she zapped herself down to the kitchen.

"Good morning, Sabrina," Hilda said when she arrived. She sat at the table reading the horoscope section of the Sunday paper.

Zelda sat across from her sister, her fingers flying across the keyboard of her laptop computer.

"I wish it was better," Sabrina said morosely. She sat at the table and pointed up a glass of orange juice and a bowl of Frosted Happy-Os.

"The carnival didn't reach the amount you'd hoped?" Zelda asked.

"No," Sabrina said. "We missed the money we needed by a little over twelve hundred dollars."

"With the storm and everything," Hilda said, "it's surprising you did as well as you did."

Sabrina poked at her cereal with the spoon. "I know, but I had hoped for more."

"You still have three weeks before the dance," Zelda pointed out. "It's too early to give up now."

"I'm not giving up." Sabrina felt even more tired and depressed talking about it. "I'm just frustrated." And the dance had never seemed farther away.

"Put it into perspective," Hilda said. "Before yesterday you were hoping for a lot more money than you made now, but now you're looking for a great deal less."

"I know, but coming up with another idea for a fund-raiser isn't going to be easy. Neither will finding people to help out with it." *Especially not with all the attention Libby's getting with her new show.*

Sabrina ate her cereal and tried not to be too down. Her aunts always worked extra hard to cheer her up when they knew she was having a rough time. But the thing she dreaded the most was when Libby found out things at the carnival hadn't gone as well as they could have.

"Look, Sabrina, all I'm saying is that Libby has already taken care of the dance," Maggie Styles said, running her fingers through her short-cropped platinum locks. "There's zero reason for us to stress ourselves out anymore trying to make the money we thought we'd need. The dance is a done deal."

Seated in the middle of the small group of students huddled in one of the private areas set aside in the Westbridge High media center on

Monday morning, Sabrina turned to face Maggie. "But what about the time we've all put in on the dance?"

"I'm with Sabrina," Amy Conrad said. Normally she was a quiet, shy redhead. "We've put a lot of time in on getting this dance arranged. And we've got some down payments out there that we may not be able to get back."

"Not all of us agreed with putting those payments down," Brad Danvers pointed out. He wore baggy skater clothes, and his hair stuck out in all directions, pale blond mixed with Kool-Aid green.

"We voted," Sabrina reminded. "Putting those payments down was what the majority agreed to do to make sure the rink, the special effects, and the caterers would be available when we needed them."

Maggie leaned forward, brushing a lock of hair out of her face. "We're not saying that what you did then was wrong. What we're saying is that we may not need to continue throwing good money after bad." Her mother ran an investment business, so she was always talking about *the bottom line.*

"Yeah," Brad said, "let's cut our losses now."

"We don't even know if that's what Libby wants to do," Eve Conklin stated. She was a slim brunette with an eye for fashion.

"Libby wasn't here when we started planning the dance," Sabrina stated. "Why does it matter now what she might want to do with the dance?"

"She's the one with the television show," Brad replied as if that was absolutely the dumbest question he'd ever heard.

"And it's not like Libby wasn't involved with the dance," Maggie objected. "While you were organizing the carnival, Libby was out there cutting deals with Channel Eight and 2 Chic By Design. She was putting in as much time getting things off the ground in her own way as you were. And who delivered the dance?"

The argument continued and Sabrina felt even worse than she had when she started out that morning. Most of the people at the meeting remained in support of Sabrina's maintaining control of the dance rather than giving in to Libby's designs, but plenty of them were hesitant about it, too.

Immediately after the meeting, Brad, Maggie, and some of the others who'd voted against continuing the dance resigned from the guidance committee. All of them had their resignations written up ahead of time and submitted them on the spot.

"Have you heard?" Valerie asked excitedly as she dropped into her seat just before the last bell that signaled the beginning of first hour.

"Heard what?" Sabrina glanced up from the sheet of paper detailing solutions for the dance financing. So far she had DANCE SOLUTIONS written at the top of the paper—neatly. That had to count for something.

"About Carla Winston," Valerie said. "She won a free makeover from Foundation's Edge."

"Cool." Sabrina was happy that someone had reason to be in a good mood today. Foundation's Edge was one of the trendiest cosmetic boutiques in Westbridge. The makeovers were incredibly expensive, and they were always booked weeks in advance.

"Even cooler," Valerie said, "Carla was able to book the makeover on the *Friday* before the dance. But what's even more exciting than that is I predicted it."

"You predicted it?"

"With the Eight-Ball Saturday night," Valerie replied. "Carla asked me if her life was going to change. I consulted the Eight-Ball. The answer came back: 'It is decidedly so.'"

"What does that have to do with the makeover?"

Valerie rolled her eyes. "What has been on the mind of every girl since Foundation's Edge has opened?"

"Well, if you put it that way, I guess that's the only answer."

"It *is* the only answer." Valerie reached into her purse and pulled the Eight-Ball out. "I'm telling you, this Eight-Ball can tell the future."

"With *yes, no,* and *maybe* answers, I guess it

can pretty much cover any situation," Sabrina admitted. "Provided you know what the situation is. Did you tell Carla she'd win the makeover?"

"Not exactly." Valerie turned around in her seat. "But she and I both knew she was thinking about a makeover at Foundation's Edge."

"Right."

"You know, you could have been a little more supportive at the moment. I'm kinda enjoying this."

Sabrina pushed out her breath as the last bell rang. "You're right. I apologize. It's just that the meeting this morning didn't go well."

"Oh, I'm so sorry," Valerie said. "I forgot all about the meeting. Carla was telling me about the phone call from Foundation's Edge this morning, and the meeting totally left my mind."

"Don't worry about it. So far we're still on track."

Mrs. Quick called the class to attention and Sabrina turned her mind to the day's schoolwork.

Harvey was waiting for Sabrina in the cafeteria at lunch, hanging back from the long line. "Hey, Sab, how's it going?"

"I missed you at the meeting this morning," Sabrina said as they went through the serving line.

"Libby called a meeting," Harvey replied. "I knew there wasn't anything I could do at your meeting this morning. So since I had a chance to go to Libby's meeting, I went there."

"Oh."

Harvey glanced at her in concern. "It was okay, wasn't it?"

"Sure," Sabrina made herself say. But it didn't feel okay and she knew it. She wished Harvey saw it that way.

"I was wondering about this Saturday," Harvey said.

Sabrina's heartbeat picked up a little. A date with Harvey always lifted her spirits. "What about this Saturday?"

Harvey shrugged and tapped his tray with a celery stick. "Since we don't have a carnival to work on, I thought maybe we'd take in a movie and maybe get a pie at the Slicery. The new Mel Gibson movie starts on Friday."

Sabrina smiled. It was hard to miss with a Mel Gibson movie. There was action for the guys, and Mel for the girls. "Sounds fab."

"Maybe after the movie, we could take in the first episode of *Real Life High.*"

"We can do that," Sabrina said, but she knew it wasn't something she'd have chosen to do.

"I talked to the others about combining the money we've got and the money we can earn in the next couple of weeks," Sabrina said, "but they weren't interested in that." She sat at the dining table in the Spellman home.

"Can you raise enough money that way?" Zelda asked, looking up from her laptap computer.

"I don't know," Sabrina answered honestly, knowing her aunt referred to Sabrina's own chronic inability to hang on to or make money at times. "If you'd asked me that two weeks ago, I'd have said, sure, no prob."

"But now?" Hilda asked.

"Now the dance committee numbers are continuing to drop." It was Friday evening now, and over half of the committee had resigned. "Even if we could raise more money, the rest of us would all be broke from donating what was left."

"And in that financial state," Aunt Louisa stated from her position hanging on the wall, "no one would be able to buy anything new to wear for the party." Aunt Louisa was a stern-looking woman in a picture frame overlooking the kitchen table. She wore a black dress and kept her hair back in a bun.

"Exactly."

"You can't fault them for not wanting to do that, Sabrina," Aunt Louisa said.

"I don't," Sabrina replied. "I know they can't just zap a new wardrobe for the dance out of thin air the way I can. The possibility of Libby being there with the television station is also stressing everybody in a major way. They want to look really good. The money they had set aside for the dance suddenly wouldn't seem like enough."

"I know you don't want to," Zelda said, "but you might start looking at Libby's arrangement with the boutique and Channel Eight a little more favorably."

"Libby didn't earn the dance," Sabrina said. "We worked for it."

"Maybe you should try to stop looking at the dance as a popularity contest," Zelda suggested.

"It's not a popularity contest," Sabrina replied. "And I haven't been looking at it that way."

Zelda gave her an *I'm-so-sure* glance. Hilda folded her arms and regarded her with raised eyebrows.

"Okay," Sabrina admitted, dropping her eyes, "maybe I have been looking at the dance like some kind of popularity contest."

"It was supposed to be a fun event," Hilda said.

"Now," Aunt Louisa said from the picture frame, "it doesn't sound like much fun at all."

"I know." The phone rang and Sabrina zapped up a handset. "Hello?"

"It's Valerie. Do you have a minute to talk?"

"Sure." Sabrina glanced at her aunts. "I'm going to take this in my room, okay?" When they nodded, she zapped herself back to her bedroom and stretched out tiredly on the bed. "What's up?"

"It happened again," Valerie said with a note of awe in her voice.

By *it*, Sabrina knew Valerie was talking about another prediction that had come true. Since Monday there'd been six altogether, but none of them had been of earthshaking consequence. One of the teachers had won five hundred dollars on a radio giveaway after Valerie had said she was coming into some money. Michelle Grayson, who'd lost a bracelet, had found it in her bedroom at home after Valerie had confirmed that's where it was. Ben Calder did well on a biology test after Valerie told him he would. The toy poodle Delaney Drake had thought lost for two weeks came home after Valerie predicted it would. Jeri Fancher had won a swim meet. And Melanie Kubasiek had found the love of her life—at least for this month.

Valerie was convinced there were others out there who had similar stories to tell, but they hadn't come forward yet.

"What happened?" Sabrina asked. She felt bad because she hadn't been able to get as excited as Valerie about her newfound fortune-telling powers.

"Do you know Taylor Butler's mom?"

Sabrina thought back but didn't think so. "No."

"She was at the carnival," Valerie said. "Taylor just called me. The guy her mother has been seeing for the last few weeks proposed at dinner tonight."

"And you predicted it?"

"Yes. Isn't that exciting?"

Sabrina tried to work up enthusiasm but couldn't. "Yes, that's great."

"You don't sound like it's great."

"I'm just worried about the dance, that's all. And I'm thinking that maybe my aunts could be right about me turning the dance into a popularity contest."

"Sabrina," Valerie said, "at our age popularity has a lot to do with anything we take part in. But that's not the reason you tried to get the dance organized. Don't forget that."

"I'll try."

"Look, I've got to go out of town with my parents for the weekend and we won't be back till late on Sunday. Why don't we have breakfast at school? My treat."

"Breakfast at school isn't necessarily a treat by any stretch of the imagination," Sabrina pointed out. "A scallion bagel to start the day isn't my idea of a good time."

"I'll bring something good." A car horn blasted at the other end of the phone connection. "Ooops. Gotta go. That's Dad."

Sabrina said good-bye and zapped the phone away. Her mind worked busily, trying to figure out some way to turn the setback with the carnival around. There had to be another way to raise the money they needed to fund the dance without Libby Chessler.

For the moment, though, the only good thing that was going on was the date with Harvey tomorrow night.

Chapter 7

☆

Sabrina's not a bad person," Libby was saying on the premiere episode of *Real Life High* Saturday night. "On the contrary, she's actually a good person. But when it comes to handling social events, she's clearly out of her depth."

"I've met her," Bob Gordon said. "She seems to be a very driven young lady."

Sitting in the tall director's chair provided by the Channel Eight studio, Libby looked elegant. She wore an off-the-shoulder black dress that flattered her figure, and wore her hair pulled back to highlight her face. Her makeup was flawless. "Most overachievers are driven," she commented.

"Sab?" Harvey said, touching her elbow.

"What?" Sabrina looked at him. They sat

together on the couch in the Spellman living room.

"We can watch something else," Harvey told her.

Sabrina forced a smile. "No, that's okay. Your part hasn't shown yet."

"I've got it taping at my house. I can watch it later."

"Don't be silly," Sabrina replied. "I can take whatever Libby dishes out." *But not without an economy-size barf bag.*

"I don't think she realizes how good you are at involving yourself in things," Harvey said. "And that bit about being an overachiever, I guess you could call it that. But I've always just thought of you as someone who really tries to get in there and get things done."

A lightning flash vented across the windowpanes just before a peal of thunder sounded ominously overhead. Electric white flooded the living room for just a moment.

"Thank you." *I need a deep breath, just so I can keep from screaming. Or pointing up something really vicious to send Libby's way.* Something with fangs and claws kept coming to mind. "Why don't I go get us a couple soft drinks and a snack? I'll be right back. Tell me if I miss anything." *Anything that* shouldn't *be missed.*

"Sure." Harvey looked uncomfortable, but he kept watching the show.

Sabrina glanced over at the recliner where Salem lay stretched out across the back. "Coming?"

Harvey glanced up at her. "I thought you wanted me to stay here."

"I do. I was talking to Salem."

"Oh."

Salem roused himself, then leaped from the chair with feline grace and padded into the kitchen.

Once inside the kitchen, Sabrina put up a silence spell over the room to make sure Harvey didn't hear her conversation with Salem. "Can you believe that show?" she asked disgustedly as she opened the cabinet doors and peered at the contents on the shelves.

Salem hopped to the island in the middle of the kitchen. "Well, it's not quite as thought-provoking as *Oprah,* doesn't have the artificial emotional impact of *Geraldo,* and lacks the violence and shocking tawdriness of *Jerry Springer.* And it will never possess the warmth of *Rosie.* The show won't last."

"And you're an expert on talk shows?" Sabrina grew even more disgusted when she realized she didn't have an idea for a quick snack. The soft drinks were covered because she'd picked them up earlier that day. She hadn't wanted to zap up Popsi Cola, Selection of the Newt Generation, or Dr. Kipper, Wouldn't You Like to Be a Kipper, Too? Harvey hadn't said anything, but the times she'd been forced to zap them up, he hadn't liked them.

"I've seen my fair share of them," Salem responded.

"I thought I heard you in here," Zelda said as she popped into the room. "Where's Harvey?"

"In the living room," Sabrina replied unhappily.

"Watching *Real Life High?*"

"Of course."

Hilda popped into the room as well. Both aunts immediately joined Sabrina in the scavenger hunt going through the kitchen cabinets. "I guess we're all stressed," Hilda said.

"You've been watching the show, too?" Sabrina asked.

Both aunts nodded.

"I've already left a message for Drell," Hilda confided. "I requested a special dispensation on your behalf for the Witches' Council to totally interfere with the programming response of the show. If he grants it, we can kill the show after tonight."

One of the earliest things Sabrina had learned about the Witches' Council was their ability to alter Nielsen ratings. However, they weren't always able to convince stars to stay with programs, which was why *Seinfeld* was no longer on.

"No," Sabrina said.

"Why not?"

"I can't believe anyone would want to listen to Libby Chessler for any length of time." At least, Sabrina hoped that was true. "I also don't think she has that much to say."

"And if you're wrong?"

"Then we'll talk to the Witches' Council."

"Good," Zelda said, "because I'm taping the show as evidence that we can use against her."

They resumed rummaging in the cabinets, not finding anything they agreed on. "Something chocolate," Hilda said.

"Chocolate-covered braised tuna," Salem interjected. "Sounds good to me." He licked his chops as the three witches turned to face him. "But maybe that's just my craving speaking."

"You can't go wrong with chocolate cake," Zelda said, pointing up a huge three-layer cake on a glass serving dish.

"With cherries?" Sabrina asked. When her aunts nodded, she zapped them into place on the cake.

"And Rocky Road ice cream," Hilda said, zapping up a gallon of it. "For those times you want to really wallow in your misery."

Zelda served, cutting thick pieces for everyone and putting them on good china. "Elegant misery."

Hilda added generous helpings of Rocky Road.

"What about me?" Salem protested. "Aren't I miserable enough?"

"Yes," all three witches answered in unison.

"Well," the cat sniffed, "that's not exactly how I meant it."

Feeling sympathetic, Sabrina quickly zapped up a dish of chocolate-braised tuna. Armed with the soft drinks and the cake and ice cream, she headed for the living room before the smell of Salem's dessert overwhelmed her.

Harvey sat hunched forward on the couch.

Glancing at the television, Sabrina noticed that the segment on at the moment had Harvey in it. She handed over the soft drink and the dessert.

"Miss anything?" she asked.

"Not much. They're introducing the group now," Harvey answered.

"What group?"

"The group Bob Gordon chose to feature as the regular ensemble."

"I didn't know there was going to be a regular ensemble," Sabrina said as she sat. "I thought the show was going to revolve around everything that went on at the high school."

"Mr. Gordon had this concept," Harvey replied. "He wants to show the high school through the viewpoints of the ensemble. So he and Libby chose nine people that they felt best represented teens today."

Like Bob Gordon and Libby Chessler would even have a clue about anything normal, Sabrina thought.

"Thanks," Harvey said, redistributing his drink and dessert.

"Why don't you introduce us to your friends, Libby," Bob Gordon said on the television set.

"Sure, Bob." Libby smiled brightly. "As for myself, I'll be your hostess each week. Again, my name is Libby Chessler. I'm the 2 Chic By Design spokesmodel, and I'm the head cheerleader at Westbridge High."

The television changed to Jill and Cee Cee, who looked almost as elegant as Libby and waved enthusiastically. "These are my friends, Jill and Cee Cee, who are going to advise us on romantic and sartorial issues." The camera returned to Libby, who smiled. "Actually, they're going to provide supplemental material to topics that I address."

Sabrina recognized the next person as Brad Forrest, Westbridge's distance-gaining halfback. He was dark, tall, and broad and had hooded eyes. And his ego was probably as big as Libby's.

"This is Brad Forrest," Libby said. "Brad has been dealing with parental pressures all his life. They've expected him to be a four-point-oh student and a major sports player. He's going to be talking to us about how those parental expectations have affected him."

Sabrina had seen Brad's parents at school functions before. Neither of them had given her the impression that they were in any way over-bearing.

Claudette Golden was next, a blue-eyed brunette with high cheekbones. "Claudette is going to be talking with us about the lack of respect for privacy that parents have for their children. She has had a number of experiences that we're going to explore."

Throughout the time Sabrina had known Claudette, it wasn't Claudette's parents that had interfered with her privacy. It was the three brothers and two sisters she had. The Golden household was a big, busy one.

"Wade Clavinski," Libby said, "who'll be talking to us about . . . a certain lack of social standing and what affect that's had on him."

Wade Clavinski ran a hand through his thick curly hair and looked embarrassed. His other hand automatically clutched his plastic pocket protector full of pens and pencils. He wore a plaid polyester shirt and wore thick-lensed glasses with heavy black rims. Though considered a geek by many at the high school, Sabrina had always found Wade to be a basically happy, if obnoxious, guy.

"Cheryl Trieste," Libby introduced the next girl, "who's going to be speaking with authority about the need for affirmation and love."

Wearing a half-shirt and skin-tight white denims that allowed a lot of tan to show, Cheryl looked straight into the camera with her turquoise eyes and smiled. Her bleached-blond hair was chopped neatly at her shoulders.

She had a history of accumulating boyfriends of other girls, then breaking their hearts just to show that she could. All the girls knew it, and all the boys seemed to forget it when they had her attention focused on them.

"Harvey Kinkle," Libby announced as the camera moved to Harvey. The on-screen Harvey tossed a nonchalant wave at the camera and smiled easily.

On the couch Harvey shook his head in embarrassment. "I look like a geek."

"You do not," Sabrina objected. "You look fine." *And you'd look even better if Libby wasn't anywhere near you.*

"Harvey's going to be talking to us about his need for acceptance," Libby said. "He's exhibited enabling tendencies."

"Harvey was one of the main supporters of Sabrina Spellman's efforts at making the carnival a success, wasn't he?" Bob Gordon asked.

"Yes, Bob," Libby answered. "That's exactly right."

"As everyone knows," the news reporter said, "the tendency to enable others is usually a sign of co-dependent behavior."

"Exactly," Libby said, "and that's one of the issues today's teen has to deal with."

"That wasn't what was said," Harvey objected. "When we were in the studio, Libby said I was going to talk about friendships."

"Obviously," Sabrina said, trying not to be unkind, "she changed her mind."

Libby went on to introduce William Poppel, an overweight young man who normally had a good disposition, who was going to discuss his weight problems as a form of rebellion against his parents. Then she introduced Ronni Bailey, a petite redhead, as a would-be social climber who wasn't really accepted in most circles.

"Sounds like an interesting ensemble you've put together, Libby," Bob Gordon said.

"An ensemble *we've* put together, Bob." Libby smiled encouragingly. "We're going to try to deal with all the teen issues that we can touch on, and inform other teens as well as parents what so many teens face during these turbulent years."

The camera tightened on Bob Gordon. "Join us next week," the newsman said, "as we bring you more of ongoing stories developing in Westbridge High. Till then, this is Bob Gordon, Channel Eight—"

The camera moved over to Libby. "—and Libby Chessler, spokesmodel for 2 Chic By Design—"

"Bringing you the real world from *Real Life High!*"

The set darkened and the credits rolled. Libby Chessler's name was prominent among them, as was Bob Gordon's.

"Man," Harvey said, "something must be wrong." His ice cream was slowly melting on his cake. "This wasn't the kind of show Libby was talking about. We were supposed to be talking about positive things."

"Well, if your idea of positive is blaming your parents, the school administration, and society for everything that goes wrong in your life," Sabrina said, "then this must be that show."

"Bob Gordon came across that way as well," Harvey said.

"The way it's set up now," Sabrina said, "they should retitle it *Libby Chessler Interviews the Seven Deadly Sins.* With a guest appearance of *Riders of the Apocalypse* as the musical guest." She was only half kidding.

Harvey glanced at her, confusion in his eyes. "I can't go along with something like this," he said. "Sab, what am I going to do?"

Hating to see him torn the way he was, Sabrina reached out and took his hand. "You're Harvey Kinkle," she said, "and you'll do the right thing. You always do." *I just don't know how Libby's going to respond when you do. But if she does anything really wicked, all bets are off. She'll get a one-way ticket to Zap City, and being a pineapple will be too good for her.*

Chapter 8

☆

I'm telling you, it really works," Valerie insisted Monday morning in the hallway at Westbridge High.

"What did you do to your head?" Sabrina asked, just noticing her friend's injury.

Valerie reached up to touch a large Band-Aid covering her right temple. She held the Magic Eight-Ball in her other hand. "I opened a car door into it."

"Are you okay?" Even under the bandage's edge, Sabrina saw the deep purple bruising spreading outward.

"I'm fine," Valerie said. "My dad told me I was only unconscious for ten or fifteen minutes."

"Unconscious?" Sabrina repeated.

Valerie nodded carefully, using her hand to

support her head. "The doctor said I might have a slight concussion. And there is this headache that I can't seem to get rid of." She cocked her head to one side. "Omigosh, we're late!" She started hurrying off, limping slightly.

Sabrina hurried after her friend. "We're not late. The bell hasn't sounded."

"I heard the bell ring," Valerie insisted. "Or maybe that was my imagination again."

"You've been hearing bells, too?" Sabrina asked. "Since you hit your head?"

"No. I mean, I was hearing them before I hit my head that time. I hit my head earlier. I just didn't knock myself out. That was new."

"You're hearing bells now?"

"Maybe. It's kinda hard to tell over that staticky noise I keep hearing."

"What staticky noise?"

"I don't know. Don't you hear it?"

"No." Sabrina noticed the dark circles under Valerie's eyes. The girl had tried to cover them with makeup that morning. When no one was looking, Sabrina pointed at Valerie and zapped her with a minor antiheadache spell that she sometimes used on herself. "How do you feel now?"

"The headache's still there. Don't worry about it. The headache will go away. What I want to show you is the Magic Eight-Ball. It really does work. Ask me a question, any question."

"Okay, how about, are you going to be well soon?" Sabrina asked.

"That won't work."

"Why not?"

Valerie shook her head gently. "I don't know. The Eight-Ball doesn't seem to answer any questions about me. Watch." She turned the Eight-Ball upside down, then flipped it back up so the round window was visible. The answer floated to the top. "'Ask again later.' That's the response I always get."

"Try it again," Sabrina said.

Turning the Eight-Ball over again, Valerie flipped it up once more. *Ask again later.* She did it six more times, and each time the same response came up.

"That's weird," Sabrina said, and a cold trickle of apprehension ran across her shoulders, prickling them. Her antiheadache spell should have worked, and there was no way the same answer would keep appearing in the Eight-Ball's window. Something was definitely wrong. "Maybe you should let me carry the Eight-Ball for a while."

Valerie snatched the Eight-Ball back out of Sabrina's reach, turning her body protectively to shield it. "No way."

"What?"

"People are starting to come up to me and ask me questions about things." Valerie's eyes were red rimmed over the dark circles. "They value what I have to tell them."

"Valerie," Sabrina said in a calm voice, "that's not your Eight-Ball. I gave it to you."

"So it's going to come down to this, is it?" Valerie asked angrily. "Well, how much do you want for it?"

"I don't want anything for it," Sabrina said.

"Good. Then it's mine. You just gave it to me."

"I did not."

"Did, too," Valerie said in a childish voice.

"Valerie, you *really* aren't being yourself right now."

"I've never felt better."

"I think you should get a second opinion."

Valerie turned the Eight-Ball over. "I'll have to ask again later." She looked at Sabrina. "You just don't understand this Eight-Ball. It really does have magic powers, Sabrina. You don't believe it because you haven't seen it happen. I have. Ask me a question."

Maybe she'll come to her senses if it gives her a wrong prediction, Sabrina thought hopefully. Glancing down the hall, she saw Cee Cee and Jill walking toward them, talking animatedly between themselves.

"Okay, fine," Sabrina said. "Here's a question: Will Cee Cee and Jill do handsprings as they go by us this morning?"

"That's a stupid question," Valerie said defensively.

"It's a question," Sabrina pointed out.

"Okay." Valerie turned the Eight-Ball over. "I'll answer it."

Sabrina pointed at the Eight-Ball and zapped it so that a positive answer would appear. *There's no way Cee Cee and Jill are going to do handsprings down the hall right now.* She felt a strange tingle as the zap left her finger.

"'It is decidedly so,'" Valerie read. She smiled broadly. "See, I told you it has magic powers."

Sabrina turned to look at the approaching cheerleaders. "Funny, I don't see any handsprings."

But without warning the two cheerleaders suddenly threw their books to one side and flipped through the hall, coming to a halt in front of Sabrina. Both girls looked at each other in disbelief; then Cee Cee cried out, "Go, Westbridge!"

"Go, Fighting Scallions!" Jill chimed in.

Some of the students in the hall started clapping and took up the cheer. Others simply made a wide berth around the cheerleaders.

Jill and Cee Cee got up quickly and retrieved their books. Then they went on their way with as much dignity as they could muster.

"I told you," Valerie announced triumphantly. "And I'll make another prediction. Will the

Harvest Moon Dance really be out of this world?"

Sabrina read the answer out loud. " 'Yes, definitely.' "

Valerie put the Eight-Ball in her purse. She smiled. "See? Everything's going to work out fine. I also know that Libby isn't going to end up in charge of the dance."

"How do you know that?"

"Because she asked me last week," Valerie said. "Of course, she thought she was only embarrassing me in front of the other people that were around."

At that moment Libby came down the hallway with the Channel Eight news crew in tow. Everyone was talking about the debut episode of *Real Life High,* although not all of the talk was favorable.

"I'll see you in class," Valerie said. "I'm going to take another aspirin and see if that helps."

"Okay," Sabrina said, watching her friend go. Then she gathered a spell and quietly mouthed it under her breath. *"Valerie's sickness I wish to be banned, so place that Eight-Ball in my hand."*

For a moment the Eight-Ball appeared to rest in her hand. She even felt the weight of it. But as she tried to close her fingers around it, the Eight-Ball disappeared. At the other end of the hall, Valerie frantically dug in her purse, then gave an evident sigh of relief.

Feeling troubled and uncertain, Sabrina forced

herself to go to her first class. Something was seriously whacked about that Eight-Ball, and she needed to find out what it was.

"You haven't seen anything yet," Libby was telling a small group of students around her as she walked down the hall. "Before this show is over, we're going to get down and dirty. We're going to talk about all the things that bother us."

Voiced encouragement came from the crowd, which made Bob Gordon following behind them grin.

All the things that bother Libby, maybe. Sabrina ignored Libby and her hangers-on, focusing on the real problem of what to do about Valerie. The girl hadn't made it completely through first hour before going to sleep.

Harvey wasn't much company at lunch. He was determined to quit Libby's show, but he felt guilty about it at the same time. And Libby had stayed so busy with everyone around her that he hadn't had the chance to tell her.

Sabrina felt bad for him, but there wasn't much she could do except offer support. She felt even worse when she excused herself from lunch early, saying she had to call home. She hoped Valerie's problem *was* something she could deal with.

In the hallway and out of sight of everyone, she zapped herself back to her bedroom in the Spellman home. Wasting no time, she pulled out

The Discovery of Magic and began thumbing through the pages, looking for the article on the Magic Eight-Ball.

A knock sounded at her door. "Sabrina," Zelda called out.

"Yes?" she replied.

"I thought I heard you zap home. Is something wrong?"

"No," Sabrina answered, thinking she could handle Valerie's problem all by herself. But then again, judging from the way Valerie looked, the problem was a big one. "Yes." However, she'd have to admit it was her fault. "Maybe."

"Oh." Zelda paused. "Maybe I could come in."

Frustrated, knowing she only had minutes before she had to get back to class, Sabrina sat on the edge of the bed and kept flipping through the pages of the book.

Zelda entered the room and gazed at the handbook, taking in Sabrina's distress. "Something *is* wrong."

"Yes." Quickly Sabrina told her about Libby scaring Jeremy Hiller away that night at the carnival, then her remembering the Magic Eight-Ball in the handbook. "I figured it would just be a prop," she finished. "Mortals can't use magical things. Can they?"

"Usually," Zelda said, looking distressed herself, "it's magical things that use mortals. Especially when we're talking about Yorbik's Magic Eight-Ball."

Sabrina cringed inside. "It's called Yorbik's Magic Eight-Ball, huh? Not simply just *an* eight-ball?"

Zelda shook her head.

"If they named it, this is really bad, isn't it?"

"Yes, I'm afraid so."

Sabrina zapped the handbook back onto the shelf it rested on. "Valerie is convinced that it can tell the future. And I saw a strange thing happen this morning myself." She elaborated, telling her aunt about Cee Cee's and Jill's impromptu cheer in the hallway. "But there's no way that was going to happen."

"No," Zelda agreed. "Yorbik's Magic Eight-Ball can't tell the future. However, it does directly influence it. Whatever wild predictions the possessor feels inclined to give, the Eight-Ball makes them come true. To some degree."

"I tried to zap it out of Valerie's purse," Sabrina said, "and I actually had my hands on it."

"But it didn't stay."

"No."

Zelda nodded. "That's part of the Eight-Ball's magic. It can't be taken from anyone who has it in their possession unless that person willingly gives it up. Or dies."

"Oooh, harsh," Sabrina said, shivering at the

thought of something happening to her friend. "Isn't there something else we can do?"

"I don't know. We'll have to talk to the person who created the Eight-Ball."

Sabrina glanced in the direction of the upstairs linen closet. "I really don't have time to take a trip to the Other Realm right now."

"Oh," Zelda said, "we don't have to go that far." She snapped her fingers.

Instantly Hilda appeared in the room, a bowling ball in one hand as she continued her approach. Then she noticed she was in Sabrina's room, not in whatever bowling alley she'd been in.

"What's the meaning of this?" Hilda demanded, resting the bowling ball on her other arm.

"Your ball?" Zelda inquired, pointing at the solid transparent crystal ball with a leaping frog trapped at its center.

"No," Hilda replied defensively. "It's one of Drell's favorites. And I was just about to beat him in the tenth frame and force him to take me out on one of those dates he's stood me up on." She raised her arm in preparation of sending herself back.

"No," Zelda said.

"No?"

"No, we have a problem."

Hilda grimaced. "There are two of you, and

you know I'm never that good at these things anyway."

"This is one that you'll be an expert on," Zelda assured her.

Hilda sighed. "All right, then." She tossed the bowling ball into the air and it vanished. Immediately Drell's laughter echoed into the room. "Oh, shut up!" Hilda said, cupping her hands so the words went wherever Drell was. She turned back to Sabrina and Zelda. "Now what's the problem?"

"Yorbik's Magic Eight-Ball," Zelda answered.

"What about it?" Hilda asked.

"Sabrina let a friend borrow it."

Hilda spun on Sabrina. "You did *what?*"

Sabrina quickly explained again.

"I should never have created that thing," Hilda stated when Sabrina had finished.

"Hilda created it when she was really young and thought she was in love," Zelda said. "Yorbik was a human, and she should have known better. Nothing against your mother, sweetheart, but the Witches' Council does have rules against such relationships for a reason."

Sabrina knew that. Not being able to see her mother for two years for fear of turning her into a ball of wax was one of the big penalties.

"Yorbik was such a nice guy in the beginning," Hilda said, remembering with a smile. "Tall and dark, with a mustache that was unruly and defiant, curled up so wickedly on the ends."

"He was a selfish cretin," Zelda stated. "His interest in Hilda increased when she told him she was a witch."

"He was a soldier when I first met him," Hilda said. "Fierce and proud. But he wanted to gain the caliph's favor, get an inside job at the palace. The rooms were so much nicer there. So I created a Magic Eight-Ball for him. They were so much better than the ones you can buy at the mall these days. I didn't know it would be so much trouble, though."

"The spell Hilda put on it helped Yorbik influence the events going on around him," Zelda said. "In less than a year Yorbik was caliph."

"Yes, and he made a grand caliph," Hilda said proudly.

"Hilda didn't like the fact that Yorbik also got the old caliph's harem," Zelda put in.

Hilda frowned. "He told me he was going to have it disbanded. He lied."

"So you took the Eight-Ball back?" Sabrina asked, wishing her aunts would get to the point.

"No," Hilda said. "Part of the magic in the Eight-Ball is that it can't be taken from the person who has it and wants it. I also couldn't destroy it later. I put it in *The Discovery of Magic* handbook because I thought it would be safe there."

"Then how did you get the Eight-Ball?" Sabrina asked. "Zelda said the person had to willingly give it up or die."

"Well," Hilda said, "Yorbik did croak. Right after I turned him into a toad. If you permanently change the possessor from being a human, the Eight-Ball is freed again as well." She smiled. "Yorbik was really surprised. Even with the Magic Eight-Ball, you can't predict everything."

"That was one of Hilda's earliest creations," Zelda said. "The Eight-Ball had a serious drawback to it. Whoever possessed it developed a really bad case of being accident prone. Rasputin had it at one point, and you know what happened to him: He was beaten, shot, strangled, poisoned, and drowned. For a time in the seventies when the Eight-Ball was missing, the Witches' Council thought President Ford had it while in office."

Sabrina was utterly bummed. *Turning one of my best friends into a frog isn't a good solution.*

"Whatever it takes, Sabrina," Zelda said, "we've got to get that Eight-Ball back into the handbook."

"Give me a little time," Sabrina pleaded. "I'll think of something."

"Don't take too long," Hilda warned. "You wouldn't believe the kind of accidents that can happen due to the Eight-Ball."

"I won't." Sabrina glanced at her watch, seeing that she had less than a minute before her next class started. "I'm going to be late. Gotta go." She zapped herself back to school, wondering how she was going to be able to get the Eight-Ball from Valerie.

And while she was doing that, she also had to come up with new ways of financing the dance and stay out of Libby's television show.

Chapter 9

☆

☆

"I quit," Harvey said that afternoon as he met Sabrina in the hallway after school.

"Quit what?" Sabrina asked. Her mind seemed as if it was going in a million different directions. The problems with the dance, the aftermath of the carnival, the financing needed to make the dance happen, Libby, and Valerie all seemed too much. For a moment she even thought Harvey was talking about quitting on them, on their relationship.

Harvey looked at her, perplexed. "I quit the show, Sab."

"Was Libby upset?"

"Yeah." A troubled expression filled his face. "I hated letting her down like that. She told me she was really counting on me."

"Quitting was the best thing you could do,"

Sabrina said as they walked down the steps toward the parking area.

"I know. Mr. Gordon was kind of upset about it, too. He said it upset the equilibrium of this week's show or something like that. Libby told him not to worry, though, because she had some stories that would be just as good as anything they had planned with me." He smiled sadly. "Kind of made me feel bad that they could do without me so quick, you know?"

Sabrina put an arm around his waist and pulled him close. "Harvey Kinkle, not everyone feels that way about you."

"I know." He draped an arm around her shoulders. "After I realized I felt bad about it awhile, then I felt stupid for feeling bad. Kinda crazy, isn't it?"

"Not really. You just don't like letting anyone down, and it was confusing because you knew in the end that the television show was a bad idea."

"Oh, I don't think the television show is a bad idea," Harvey disagreed. "Libby's got a lot of good ideas. It's just that I don't think I was the right guy to be on it."

"Let's go to the Slicery," Sabrina suggested. "I'll help you drown your sorrows in a frosted mug of root beer." *And while we're at it, maybe I'll drown my own for a little while.*

As it turned out, Harvey wasn't the only person to quit *Real Life High.* Half the original cast members never made it back for the second show. Libby's demands and the direction the show was taking offended a number of people.

But the school continued to talk about the show, and Bob Gordon talked to Libby about the increasing number of businesses interested in buying advertising time on the fledgling show. Sabrina knew about it because she eavesdropped on their conversations. Plus, Libby wasn't shy about telling everyone at Westbridge High.

Sabrina also kept an eye on Valerie, who was becoming increasingly accident prone. Scrapes and bruises seemed to multiply hourly. Coach Petersen in gym even got to the point that he wouldn't let Valerie on anything above floor level, afraid that she would fall again.

Valerie continued to tell fortunes, and small miracles continued to happen as a result of it. No one really thought the good fortune was brought about by the Eight-Ball except for Valerie, but a number of people liked having their fortunes told.

Sabrina considered scheme after scheme for getting the Eight-Ball away from Valerie, but none of them seemed workable. In the meantime, Hilda and Zelda kept putting pressure on her to do *something*.

But by the time Saturday rolled around, all Sabrina had really managed to do was arrange another date with Harvey.

* * *

"There's going to come a time," Zelda warned that Saturday night, "when Valerie makes a prediction that's going to have cataclysmic repercussions if you don't get that Eight-Ball out of her hands."

"I'm working on it," Sabrina said as she took a carton of caramel popcorn from the pantry. "I've stolen the Eight-Ball twice only to have it mysteriously reappear in Valerie's locker each time. Both times she was frantic about where she might have lost it. I felt really sorry for her."

"You'll get over feeling sorry when you wake up one morning and find out that the human race has been replaced by mushrooms as the most intelligent species," Hilda responded.

"That wouldn't happen," Sabrina said, pouring the caramel popcorn into a serving bowl. "Would it?"

"It could. That Eight-Ball is very powerful. I was young enough at the time that I didn't really know what I was doing. The very fact that I can't *uncreate* it should tell you something."

"Where did you get the caramel corn?" Salem protested, looking up from his resting place on the kitchen island.

"The pantry," Sabrina said.

"I looked in there earlier and I didn't see it," the cat argued.

"That's because I know how much you love caramel corn," Sabrina said. "And if you'd had all day at it, you would have eaten the whole carton by now. So I turned it invisible and odorless. Until now." She poured a handful in a smaller bowl and put it in front of the cat. That gave her an idea. "Hey, what if I turn the Eight-Ball invisible to Valerie?"

Hilda shook her head. "Won't work. I fixed it so that any attempt to turn it invisible will fail. It will automatically reveal itself to the person who possesses it." She smiled in spite of the circumstances. "It was the first real object of power I made, and it's lasted hundreds of years."

"I wouldn't be so proud," Zelda admonished.

The smile fell from Hilda's face. "Right."

Sabrina took soft drinks from the refrigerator and headed back to the living room where Harvey was.

Harvey sat on the couch, tense as he watched television. The second episode of *Real Life High* was supposed to come on in the next few minutes.

Sitting beside him, Sabrina felt the tiredness from the last few days fill her. She'd canvased the school trying to find new fund-raising ventures to get the final eight hundred dollars they needed to finish paying for the dance. They'd made another four hundred from a combination carwash and bake sale. And she'd tried to get the Eight-Ball from Valerie while dodging Libby and the Channel Eight film crew.

"Hey, thanks," Harvey said, taking the bowl of caramel popcorn from her.

Sabrina only nibbled at the popcorn, finding her appetite just wasn't up to it. She was worried about too many things. It looked as if Libby had won, and Valerie had lost. And Sabrina hadn't been good enough to prevent either.

Then *Real Life High* came on, rolling through the teaser of Libby telling everyone she had a secret. The credits followed, finally opening up on the evening's show by focusing on Bob Gordon.

"Welcome to another edition of *Real Life High,*" the newscaster said, "where we let you in on some of the problems and challenges facing today's teenager. I'm Bob Gordon, with Channel Eight News. With me tonight is your hostess, Libby Chessler, who is also the 2 Chic By Design spokesmodel."

"Thank you, Bob," Libby said. "I'm happy to be here. I have quite a show lined up for you tonight."

Bob Gordon hesitated just a beat too long, but never quite lost the professional smile. "Yes, I'm sure *we* do have quite a show lined up."

"No doubt about it," Libby went on, "one of the most enjoyable but challenging aspects about being young is trying to follow the course of true love."

"That's never an easy course to follow at any age," Bob Gordon replied. "There are so many pitfalls along the way."

Libby looked annoyed that the newscaster

interrupted her. "The cruelest twist of fate, though, can put the wrong people together. I mean, you just know you're right for some guy, but he's only got eyes for some loser that doesn't even come close to competing with you when you're having your worst day ever."

Sabrina got the distinct impression that Libby was venting about Harvey's and her relationship.

"I see what you mean, Libby," Bob Gordon stated, though it was apparent to Sabrina that the newscaster didn't get it at all.

Libby ran a hand through her hair, smoothing it back into place as she regained her composure. "I'd like to introduce you to two of tonight's guests."

"As you may have noticed during the opening credits," Bob Gordon said, "our cast has been downsized."

"But only so that we could bring you important stories more in depth," Libby said. "We had to clear some deadwood to make room for the good stuff."

Bob Gordon winced.

"They shot this episode this morning," Harvey commented. "I overheard Jill and Cee Cee talking about it at the Slicery when I picked up the pizza to bring over here."

The date tonight had been a simple one, consisting of the pizza and a video Sabrina had rented.

"So they didn't have time for retakes," Sabrina said.

Harvey shook his head. "Also, Libby rewrote the entire script. Mr. Gordon kind of had to ad-lib his way through the whole thing. From what I heard, he wasn't very happy about it. He expected to keep creative control of the show's direction."

That was Bob Gordon's second mistake, Sabrina thought. *His first was in going along with Libby.*

"This is Logan Powell and Madison Lockwood," Libby said, waving to the young couple seated to her left.

Sabrina recognized Logan and Madison from around Westbridge High, though she'd never really gotten chummy with either of them. Logan was a pitcher on the baseball team and was broad shouldered and good-looking in a roguish kind of way, with sandy blond hair that hung down into his eyes. His smile was crooked and daring.

Madison was curvy and wore her dark hair cut short and off her face. She had on a kelly-green turtleneck, which clung to her figure, with designer overalls.

"These two lovebirds have been dating for nearly three months, isn't that right?" Libby asked.

Madison nodded proudly and took one of

Logan's hands in both of hers. "That's right, Libby." She grinned.

"Logan's a good-looking guy, isn't he?" Libby asked.

Logan smirked and waved at the camera.

Uh-oh, Sabrina thought.

"Bet it broke a lot of hearts out there when you decided Madison was the one-and-only girl for you," Libby told Logan.

Still smiling, Logan shifted in his seat. "Well, I don't know about that, but I know there were more than a few who couldn't believe I'd settled down."

"What about you, Madison?" Libby asked. "Were you surprised when Logan settled down?"

Madison shook her head, grinning. "No. Not really. What we have between us is real. Not that kid stuff that we've all experienced."

"Then maybe Logan can explain this," Libby said, pointing.

The camera view abruptly cut to last Friday night's football game.

"Madison, didn't Logan call you and tell you he couldn't go out last night?" Libby asked.

"That's right. He was sick. He said he was worried about doing your show."

"Well, he must have gotten to feeling better," Libby said, "because there he is in the stands at last night's football game."

The camera tightened up its focus on the audience, revealing Logan in sharp relief. He wasn't alone. He had his arm draped over the girl next to him, sitting cozily. And she definitely wasn't Madison.

"What?" Madison screeched as the camera cut back to her. She turned to Logan. "What were you doing there with Heidi Weiss?"

Logan looked as if he didn't know what to do. He pushed back in his chair from Madison as far as he could.

"I think we can answer that question," Libby replied. The camera view shifted into halves. One of them continued to roll on Logan and Madison in the television station, and the other showed more footage from the football game. A moment longer and Logan twisted around to kiss the girl he was with.

"You two-timing, unfaithful loser!" Madison shrilled. "How could I have ever believed you when you said that you loved me?" She took a ring off her finger and threw it at Logan, then removed a necklace as well.

"It's not what you think!" Logan protested, protecting himself from the thrown objects. But the frozen still of him kissing Heidi Weiss remained in the background behind him.

"I think we'll take a short commercial break," Bob Gordon said, getting out of his chair to avoid the flying missiles. "We'll be right back to *Real Life High!*"

"Wow," Harvey said, hand poised over the

caramel popcorn bowl. "Now that I had *not* heard about."

"Libby shouldn't have done that," Sabrina said, almost not believing the girl had stooped so low.

"I don't think it was her," Harvey said as a 2 Chic By Design commercial played. Libby modeled some of the winter fashions now on sale at the boutique. "The television show producers must have put her up to that."

"How would they have known about Logan and Madison?" Sabrina asked. She knew that Harvey just didn't want to believe Libby could be as unscrupulous as she was. He had trouble believing anyone was bad.

"I don't know," Harvey answered. "The film crew has been around campus a lot."

"The chances of them knowing about Logan and Heidi are even smaller," Sabrina pointed out.

"Yeah. I guess so. But maybe Libby thought she was just helping them. Or helping Madison at any rate."

The show came back on before Sabrina could argue. As it continued, she realized that convincing Harvey of Libby's duplicitous nature wasn't her responsibility.

Madison and Logan were gone from the set. Libby had changed clothes, and Bob Gordon appeared stressed in a major way.

"If you're just joining us," Bob Gordon said, "welcome to *Real Life High,* with your hosts Libby Chessler—"

"And Bob Gordon," Libby finished in a rush. "But enough of that. Let's get to our next story. Meet Barry Whisten, another student at Westbridge High."

Sabrina remembered Barry from a physics class last semester. He was quiet and shy, good-looking but not too athletic. His fair hair was parted and combed neatly into place. He wore an Oxford button-down and khaki slacks.

"Hi, Barry," Libby said warmly. "It's nice to have you here."

"It's nice to be here," Barry responded politely.

Evidently he didn't see what happened to Logan and Madison, Sabrina thought.

"Do you know why you're here, Barry?" Libby asked.

"Because you invited me," Barry replied, grinning uncertainly.

"Well, that's one good reason."

"And I thought maybe we were going to talk about some of the science programs I've been invited to participate in at two colleges next summer," Barry said, but it came across sounding like a question.

"That is so off-base," Libby said. "We're going to talk about the importance of first impressions. You're familiar with those, aren't you?"

"Well, yes. To get into those college programs, I had to talk to—"

"Barry," Libby interrupted, "we're not here to talk about those college programs. We're here to talk about that blind date you had last week. You remember, the one that you had with Tina Langstrom, who goes to another high school across town. Your mother set up that date, didn't she?"

Barry hesitated, then finally said yes. His cheeks blazed furious crimson.

"Libby," Bob Gordon said, "what are you doing?"

"Illustrating a point," Libby answered. "The social lives of teens are so dramatic, so much pressure is put on them to put their best foot forward. I just wanted to see it in action. When I heard about Barry's blind date with Tina, I seized the opportunity."

Barry looked increasingly uncomfortable, glancing around as if he might bolt at any second.

"You wanted this show to be about issues real teens deal with," Libby said. "That's what I'm doing." She turned her attention back to Barry, leaning forward conspiratorially. "How did your mom set up your blind date?"

"Uh, she met Tina's mom at the bank," Barry said, pulling at his collar and staring at the camera as if it were hypnotizing him. "My mom works there and Tina's mom banks there."

"Charming, I'm sure," Libby said. "How did you feel about your mom setting up a blind date for you?"

"I don't know. I was nervous," Barry hurried on. "But Tina was such a nice girl."

"Has your mom set up dates for you before?"

"Yes."

"How do you feel about that?"

"I don't know."

Sabrina felt sorry for Barry being put on the spot the way he was. It took a real effort not to switch the television off. This was bad, even for Libby.

"Does your mom know what kind of social stigma can be attached to someone who dates an underclassman?" Libby asked.

"I don't know."

"And it is true that while you're a senior, Tina is only a *freshman.*" Libby made it sound like a social disease.

"Yeah, I guess so." Barry continued pulling at his collar. "She seemed like a really nice girl."

"Would you like to know how Tina felt about you?" Libby asked. Before Barry could answer, she turned to the camera. "Roll the tape."

The camera panned in on a slim blond with big blue eyes and a really cute smile. The problem was, she *looked* like a freshman. And Sabrina knew that was the kiss of death. Barry was in for tons of ridicule and teasing.

"Hi," Tina said nervously, waving at the camera. She was dressed in a short red mini, not at all a match for Barry's conservative image.

"Can you tell us what your first impression of Barry Whisten was?" Libby asked, off-camera.

"He was kind of a geek, really," Tina said. "Polite and everything, and nice, but still a geek. There's no disguising that." She paused. "Oh, and his hands felt really clammy. He tried holding hands with me at the movie, but I told him I thought I had poison ivy. It almost grossed me out."

The camera view blinked, then refocused on the studio. Barry Whisten's chair was empty. Libby turned to Bob Gordon. "Barry had to go," she announced, "but I think we can safely point to a few problems that teens encounter in the dating world." She ticked them off on her fingers. "First impressions are so important. Blind dates really aren't all that much fun. And having your mom organize your social life shouldn't be done at all."

The show only got worse from there. Bob Gordon held on like a man trapped on a runaway roller coaster, finally giving up any attempt at co-hosting the show. It was Libby's production all they way.

Finished with Barry Whisten, she called Tim and Tucker, the Harris twins, onstage. In a few short minutes she reduced them to fighting like two-year-olds over conversations each of them had had about the other. Sibling rivalry exploded across the television screen, first in yelling voices, then in actual pushing and shoving.

When the show was over, Sabrina sat in stunned disbelief. No matter how bad she'd thought things would get with Libby running her own television show, Sabrina had never thought they'd get this bad.

Chapter 10

"Channel Eight and 2 Chic By Design canceled Libby's show," Valerie said, rushing up to Sabrina's locker.

It was Monday morning and Sabrina hadn't rested well over the weekend. The dance was only a week away and they still needed over seven hundred dollars to pay for everything. "What?"

"*Real Life High*," Valerie said. "They canceled it after Saturday. Libby just got word about it this morning. Of course, some of the other kids knew about it because their parents called in and complained about the show. Channel Eight assured them that there wouldn't be any more episodes, and apologies are going out to all the people Libby slammed Saturday night."

Sabrina felt cheered by the good news, then noticed that one of Valerie's arms was in a sling. "What happened to your arm?"

"I fell getting out of the car last night," Valerie answered. "The doctor in the emergency room said it was just a really bad sprain. It should be okay in a few days."

"I hope so."

Valerie nodded. "It will. I'm getting to know injuries. This one wasn't as bad as it could have been."

But it still wouldn't have happened without that Eight-Ball being around. Sabrina felt guilty.

"The really bad news is the Harvest Moon Dance," Valerie said. "It got canceled, too. Channel Eight and 2 Chic By Design both said that Libby didn't live up to her agreement. After Saturday night, sponsors for the show dropped out."

"Then the only chance we have to make the dance happen is if we can get the money to fund it," Sabrina said.

"How much do we need?"

"A little more than seven hundred dollars." Sabrina thought furiously, but nothing came to mind. She felt so frustrated. "Are you sure it's canceled?" Now it wasn't about *who* actually put the dance together. It was about whether it would actually happen. That put things in a lot different perspective.

"The dance is going to happen," Valerie said.

"Remember? The Eight-Ball predicted that it would."

That, however, didn't cheer Sabrina up. Especially with Valerie standing there with her arm in a sling.

By that afternoon the whole school knew about Libby's show getting canceled. Libby's response was that she was taking the show to other markets, that Channel Eight obviously didn't know how to back a winner, and that losing *Real Life High* was going to be bigger than they ever imagined.

Sabrina passed up the opportunity to throw verbal barbs at Libby. The girl had caused herself enough problems. Instead, Sabrina concentrated on figuring out ways of getting the necessary funding. Short of pointing up a miracle, though, she didn't know how she was going to accomplish that. Magic wasn't an answer this time.

As she walked home from school, a scary thought hit her. If the Eight-Ball's predictions always came true because it influenced events, then how was it going to make sure the dance happened the way it predicted? Valerie had said the dance was going to take place and "be out of this world."

Unless Sabrina found a way to get the Eight-Ball from Valerie's possession, there was no telling what it might do to further complicate things.

At the Spellman home her aunts weren't much help, either. Not feeling like conversation, Sabrina went to her room, saying she had a lot of studying to do. Instead, she lay in bed and tried very hard not to think about all the things that had gone wrong.

Salem came to join her, griping about the diet Hilda and Zelda had him on again. He pounced onto the bed and settled in, wrapping his tail around himself.

"So they canceled Libby's show, did they?" he asked.

"Yes. And the dance," Sabrina replied.

"Well, that's too bad about the dance, but I'm sure going to miss that show. With the way Libby was starting to treat her guests, things were beginning to get really interesting. I had the feeling after watching Saturday night that there might be a censored version on videotape soon."

"That's not funny."

The cat looked at her with wide eyes. "I was serious. Channel Eight weenied out on what could have been a classic. Histrionics. Mayhem. Name-calling. With luck, maybe even a little eye-gouging. Reminded me of France's first congress. Ah, those were the days."

Sabrina ignored him.

"But it does sort of make you wonder what they're going to put on in its place." Salem sighed. "Of course, it'll never be as good as watching Libby work a crowd."

Sabrina sat up in bed as his words sparked an idea. "What?"

"I said, I wonder what they'll put on in the show's place," Salem repeated. "I guess they could move the creature feature back an hour."

"The advertisers Channel Eight was starting to attract locally aren't going to be thrilled with that solution," Sabrina said. "Salem, you're a brainiac! You've just given me a great idea!" Her mind raced hurriedly. She pointed at the phone and said a quick spell that would connect her to Drew Fontaine, the owner of 2 Chic By Design.

The phone rang twice. "Fontaine," a masculine voice answered.

"Mr. Fontaine," Sabrina said, willing herself to be calm. She got out of bed and started to pace, lining up her thoughts.

"Who is this?" Fontaine asked irritably. "And how did you get the number to my car phone?"

"My name is Sabrina Spellman. I attend Westbridge High."

"Look," Fontaine said sharply, "if this is going to be another threat about a lawsuit, my attorneys are—"

"It's not a threat, Mr. Fontaine," Sabrina said. "I'm calling about an offer."

"An offer for what?"

"You canceled *Real Life High,*" Sabrina said.

"Yes."

"I think it was the best thing you could have done at the time," Sabrina said.

"I didn't have a choice after Saturday."

"No, you didn't. But you also killed our chances for the Harvest Moon Dance that was planned."

"I can't be held accountable for that," the boutique owner said.

"I wasn't even going to try. But I do have something to offer."

"I'm listening. I've made a lot of good business deals by listening, Miss Spellman."

"How would you like to sponsor the Westbridge Harvest Moon Dance anyway?" Sabrina asked. She hurried on before Fontaine could reply. "I'm not talking about a talk show or teen issues. I'm thinking of live footage shot at the dance, with commercials advertising the clothing line you carry in your boutique."

"I don't know."

"Parents can tune in that night to see their kids having a good time instead of being attacked on television," Sabrina pointed out. "Imagine all the VCRs in the area that will record the dance. Including the commercials for 2 Chic By Design. How many copies of that do you think will be circulated around Westbridge? How many times do you think those commercials will be watched over and over again in the next few weeks?"

Fontaine laughed. "Miss Spellman, I like the way you think. How much money are we talking about for the rights to do something like that?"

"A little over seven hundred dollars," Sabrina said.

"That's cheap enough," the boutique owner said. "Tell me what you have in mind."

Sabrina did, feeling her heart pound against her ribs with every word she spoke. She was so nervous. But when she finished, Fontaine agreed with everything she said.

"I like the idea," the man said. "And getting back some of the community's goodwill at this point *is* extremely attractive."

"I don't know if Channel Eight will go along with broadcasting the dance," Sabrina said. "They do have a creature feature they can run."

"Bob Gordon *and* Channel Eight owe me," Fontaine replied. "I'll make them see things my way. Consider yourself in the dance business, Miss Spellman. I'll be calling you tomorrow to set up the specifics."

"Thank you," Sabrina said. She hung up the phone. Then she pumped her arm into the air. "Yes. YES. *YESSSS!*" She reached down and picked Salem up.

"Hey, watch out," the cat protested. "You're going to wrinkle the fur."

"Supply and demand," Sabrina said. "Who'd have thought a business class would have helped make the dance a reality? Mr. Fontaine thinks advertising during the dance is going to be one of the best things that ever happened. He wanted better programming to capture the attention of the teen viewers, and the dance is going to do exactly that." She zapped downstairs to tell her aunts the good news.

"That's great, Sabrina," Zelda said when she finished. "However, you've still got to deal with Yorbik's Magic Eight-Ball."

"I'll do it," Sabrina said. Even being reminded of that problem didn't bring her completely down. "Things are turning around now. Just give me a couple more days."

"Well, you're the heroine of Westbridge High," Harvey said as he skated with Sabrina Saturday night. He held her hand warmly in his, taking away the chill coming off the ice rink. "You made the Harvest Moon Dance happen." He waved his free hand at the laser light show going on around them. Fog created by dry ice misted over a wild assortment of aliens, monsters, and science-fiction movie characters. "And it's just the way you wanted it to be."

And it really was, Sabrina had to admit. To

make things even better, Libby had refused to come to the dance, staging a protest of her own.

Harvey wore a maroon Captain Starr uniform from one of the *Space Journey* movies, complete with jetpack. Sabrina dressed like Teila, Captain Starr's love interest in the movies. Her evening gown was a diaphanous white mini that hinted at the one-piece pale cerulean bodysuit underneath. She accessorized it with jade earrings and a jade headband that echoed the greenish make-up she wore to make her look as though she'd been descended from dragons the way the Teila character had been.

"I'd settle for dancing with you," Sabrina said, twisting so that she was skating backward through the crowd of Westbridge students.

Harvey held her close, laughter sparkling in his eyes.

"What's so funny?" she asked.

"You."

"You mean the way I look like Teila, Dragon Princess of the Stars? I thought you liked that look."

"I do like that look," Harvey said. "I'm just laughing because I can see how happy you are, that's all. You've been so worried for weeks, and there wasn't anything I could do for you. I'm just glad you're happy now."

"Thank you, Harvey. But part of the reason that I'm so happy is because I'm here with you." Sabrina continued skating and dancing.

Drew Fontaine had gone above and beyond what had been necessary to ensure the dance's success. The light show was nothing short of terrific, and the catering tables were kept fully stocked even in the presence of teens.

The ice rink was so crowded it looked as if nearly all of Westbridge High had turned out for the dance. There was no doubt that it was going to be called one of the year's greatest successes.

The only downer was seeing Valerie standing at rink side with her arm in the sling. She didn't trust herself out on the ice. Sabrina still hadn't managed to get Yorbik's Magic Eight-Ball away from her.

Channel Eight filmed the dance with three cameras, providing full coverage that was going out live for the night. They'd also nixed the creature feature altogether for the night, intending to show the dance for a full two hours because of local sponsor interest.

Nothing could go wrong.

Then the floor seemed to tilt for one crazy instant, and Sabrina's stomach turned threateningly the way it sometimes did in elevators that dropped too fast.

"What was that?" Harvey asked. "It felt like we just dropped through the floor."

A few of the skaters had fallen and were getting back up.

"I don't know," Sabrina said. "It seemed like an earthquake." Then she noticed Zelda waving to her. Both she and Hilda had volunteered to be chaperones for the evening. The look on her aunt's face told her it was serious. "Uh, Harv, why don't I go see what my aunt wants, and I'll get back to you?"

"Okay."

Sabrina skated through the happy crowd, looking at all the smiling faces and trying not to worry prematurely because her aunt was frowning. "What's wrong?"

"Did you just feel that?" Zelda asked. Hilda joined them, looking somewhat dismayed herself.

"Sure," Sabrina said. "It was some kind of tremor or something, but nothing to really be worried about. Right?"

"Wrong," Hilda said. She took Sabrina's arm and guided her to the ice rink's front doors. "There's a lot to be worried about."

The front doors had been covered with black cloth to keep the laser show's effects sharp and clean.

"Take a look outside," Hilda urged, pulling a corner of the cloth to one side.

Sabrina peered outside the double set of glass doors. Instead of the parking lot and the street that normally faced Happy's Ice Rink, only a landscape of jagged, barren rock stretched out in front of her. She didn't know what it was she was looking at, but she was certain she was no place she'd been before!

Chapter 11

"What happened?" Sabrina asked, quickly covering up the strange landscape outside Happy's Ice Rink before anyone could see it. Just before she covered the view, she saw the glimmering of a huge orange-yellow ball hanging in the black of space to the right.

"Yorbik's Magic Eight-Ball," Hilda said. "It's the only thing that could have done this. I'm really sorry to mess up the dance like this, Sabrina."

"You didn't do it," Sabrina said. "I should have read the warning about the Eight-Ball." She took a deep breath. "Okay, I'm assuming we're not in Westbridge anymore. Or maybe we're just not there at a time when it exists." She'd recently been introduced to time travel and all the paradoxes that it presented when she and Salem had been placed on trial in old West Bridge.

"No," Zelda said, "we're in our proper space-time continuum." She consulted a pocket computer she took from her purse. "However, we're not on Earth anymore."

Valerie's words echoed in Sabrina's mind. *"Will the Harvest Moon Dance really be out of this world?"* "Yes, definitely," Sabrina said.

"What?" Hilda asked.

"Just remembering," Sabrina said. "If we're not on Earth, then where are we?"

"As nearly as I can figure," Zelda replied, "we're on Callisto."

"Callisto?" The name sounded vaguely familiar to Sabrina, but she couldn't place it. There was so much geography to learn, especially when she had to include places in the Other Realm.

"The second largest moon orbiting Jupiter," Zelda said.

"Jupiter?" Sabrina couldn't believe it. "How can we be on Jupiter? There aren't any electrical hookups. None of the power would be on in here."

"There also isn't a breathable atmosphere," Zelda pointed out.

"You're forgetting about Yorbik's Magic Eight-Ball," Hilda said. "I really did a good job of putting that thing together. It transferred us here, kept the power going, and made the atmosphere breathable. I fixed it so that no matter what silly prediction Yorbik made to the caliph, it would come true. And Yorbik had a really wild imagination, let me tell you."

The door to the office suddenly opened and Mr. Copeland, the owner of Happy's Ice Rink stepped out. "Sabrina, is anything wrong out here?"

Sabrina shrugged and smiled. "Not that I know of, Mr. Copeland. The dance seems to be going along just fab."

Mr. Copeland didn't appear certain. He walked to the front doors and lifted the material to peer out.

Reacting quickly, Zelda raised a hand and said, *"Float like a butterfly, hum like a bee, let him see what he thinks he should see."*

"Hmmm," Mr. Copeland said, dropping the material. "That's got to be the strangest thing I've ever seen."

"What?" Sabrina asked helpfully.

"CNN is covering the dance here in West-bridge," Mr. Copeland said.

"What?" Sabrina exploded.

"Well, come in and see for yourself." Mr. Copeland waved Sabrina and her aunts into the office and pointed at the small TV on the desk that nearly filled the tiny room.

Sure enough, the CNN logo showed in the corner of the screen. And footage from Westbridge's Harvest Moon Dance played on the screens.

"Most bizarre occurrence NASA spokespeople are saying the administration has ever seen," the CNN anchorwoman reported. "To repeat this hour's top story, it seems that a Voyager-class space probe in orbit around Jupiter on an exploratory mission is receiving an electronic broadcast from Callisto, the second largest of the planet's moons."

Footage of the dance rolled on the CNN big screens, showing dozens of aliens, monsters, and movie characters mixed in with some West-bridge High students who hadn't dressed up for the occasion.

"That's us all right," Mr. Copeland said. "Because that's exactly what you're seeing out there."

"Allowing a few minutes' lag time," Zelda said.

Everyone looked at her.

"Well," she said, "it is approximately three hundred ninety million miles away from Earth at its closest and four hundred eighty million miles away at its farthest. I don't really know where we are in relation to each other at the moment. But this isn't one of those science-fiction movies. Telecommunications are limited by speed."

Mr. Copeland studied the images on the television more closely, then peered out his window overlooking the ice rink floor. "I think you're right. That's not the same image as I'm seeing out there." He flipped stations over to Channel Eight. "But look here. This broadcast isn't the same, either."

"That's because magic is faster than telecommunications," Zelda announced. "We're getting all the signals from Earth just as though we were there. That's how Johnny Depp got to be such a big star in the Orion cluster."

"Magic?" Mr. Copeland said. "Now you're not making any sense at all. I—"

Sabrina pointed at the man and froze him into place. "When I start him up again," she said, "I'll remove everything we've said from his memory."

"That's not the hard part," Hilda pointed out as she changed the channel back to CNN. "You've got to get Yorbik's Magic Eight-Ball from your friend."

"NASA scientists don't have an explanation for how their robot probe is picking up the broadcast signals," the anchorwoman went on. "But there's a lot of tension in the control room in Houston at this moment. In approximately ten minutes the probe will be within range to start transmitting pictures back to Earth that scientists can study."

"That's definitely not cool," Sabrina said.

"There is the chance they won't be able to spot

us," Zelda said. "Callisto has a diameter of over three thousand miles. That translates into a large surface area."

"NASA believes it has a lock on the origin of the broadcast," the CNN anchorwoman said. "And the side that the broadcast is coming from will be visible to the probe's long-range sensors."

"Sabrina," Hilda said more fiercely, "you've got to get Yorbik's Magic Eight-Ball. *Fast!* Once Valerie no longer has it, Zelda and I can put the ice rink back in Westbridge."

"And hope that no one has noticed it's missing." Zelda pointed at Sabrina's wrist and a watch appeared there. It was counting down from nine minutes and thirty-seven seconds.

"Okay," Sabrina said. "I'm going, I'm going." She walked back out into the main area of the ice rink, wondering how she was going to handle getting the Eight-Ball out of Valerie's hands.

The dance was in full swing. Rock music thundered from the ceiling and walls. The light show strobed the darkness, creating all kinds of kaleidoscopic images that burned in the air for long seconds.

Sabrina considered freezing everyone in place, but the Channel Eight cameras would have transmitted that. And that would have been as hard to explain as the ice rink's presence on one of Jupiter's moons. *Well, maybe not quite.*

She watched Harvey briefly, enjoying how cute he looked in his Captain Starr uniform, skimming across the ice with surefooted grace. Then she walked over to Valerie, who held on to the railing by the rink.

"You're not skating," Sabrina said. The watch on her wrist hit the eight-minute mark.

"No," Valerie said. "As awkward as I've been lately, I don't think I can chance ending up with two sprained arms." She held up her injured limb in its sling.

"Do you still think that Eight-Ball is telling futures correctly?" Sabrina asked.

"Yes." Valerie smiled, and the expression lit up her face in spite of the dark circles under her eyes.

"I have a question for it."

"Okay." Valerie dug the Eight-Ball out of her purse.

"Ask it if I'm on one of Jupiter's moons at this very minute," Sabrina instructed.

"That's pretty strange."

"Humor me."

Valerie turned the Eight-Ball upside down, then righted it. "'Yes,'" she read. "Yes?" She shook the Eight-Ball. "That doesn't make any sense."

"See?" Sabrina asked. "That's what I've been trying to tell you. The Eight-Ball hasn't been telling people's fortunes. You have."

"I have?"

"Sure," Sabrina said. "You must have tapped

into some paranormal power you've had all along."

Valerie cradled the Eight-Ball protectively as skaters moved around her. "Even so. That power never manifested itself till I had the Eight-Ball. It might still be some kind of trigger."

No! Sabrina screamed silently inside her own mind. "I think you're obsessing on the Eight-Ball."

"Obsess? Me?" Valerie forced a laugh. "I don't obsess on things."

Sabrina just looked at her.

"Okay, maybe I obsess on a few things," Valerie admitted. "But I don't obsess on Eight-Balls."

"Have you ever had one before?" Sabrina's watch showed five minutes twenty-three seconds left till the robot probe got into view.

"When I was a kid," she replied. "But it never worked as well as this one."

"You're obsessing about this one," Sabrina stated.

"No, I'm not. And I think I'm through talking to you about this." Valerie turned on her heel and walked away.

"What?" Sabrina called out, startled. Valerie would *never* just walk away from her like that. She started after her friend, conscious of the time slipping away.

Valerie went into the bathroom and stopped in

front of a sink. She rummaged in her purse and came up with a makeup case.

"We need to talk," Sabrina said.

"I don't think so." Valerie tried in vain to hide the dark circles under her eyes.

"Do you still have that headache?"

"It's never gone away," Valerie admitted. "But I've gotten kind of used to it."

"The headache is because of your obsession with the Eight-Ball," Sabrina said. Less than three minutes remained.

"How can you say that?" Valerie demanded angrily.

"Because I've never seen you this obsessed about anything before," Sabrina replied. Other girls moved to the sinks around them. "This has gotten to the point that it's unhealthy."

Valerie ignored her.

Knowing she was going to have to do something drastic to convince her friend to change her mind, Sabrina pointed at the mirror in front of Valerie. The enchantment was placed so that only she and Valerie could see it. Sabrina felt really sorry about what was going to happen. If the circumstances hadn't called for something so drastic, she'd never have done what she was about to do.

Valerie's image in the mirror began to wither. The skin stretched tight across her skull, plastering harder than hot wax. Her teeth showed against her too-tight, too-small lips. The dark circles under her eyes dropped, sagging past her cheekbones to the corners of her mouth. Then her eyes erupted from her head on stalks that turned out to be twisting snake-things.

Sabrina was almost grossed out herself. She drew on the demented inspiration given to her from last Saturday night's creature feature after *Real Life High*.

Valerie's eyes danced sort of a conga on her sharp, bony cheeks, swaying on top of the snaky bodies. Then the eyes both turned to Eight-Balls, the pupils forming the answer window.

"Is this how you want things to be?" Sabrina whispered.

Abruptly both windows in Valerie's Eight-Ball eyes filled up with the predictions that read *Ask Again Later*.

Valerie yelped in fear, blinking her eyes.

Sabrina glanced at the watch Zelda had given her. Fifty-seven seconds remained. And that was how long she had before she either turned Valerie permanently into a toad, or allowed her secret to come out into the open.

Valerie dug into her purse and handed Sabrina the Eight-Ball. "Here. Take this. I never want to see it again!"

Sabrina felt the pulse of magic in the Eight-Ball now that she knew what it was. "I'll be right back," she promised Valerie as the other girl sat down by the sink. "I'll go see if Mr. Copeland has some aspirin in his first-aid kit."

Sabrina, the Teenage Witch

"I'm not moving," Valerie promised, holding her hands over her eyes.

Sabrina pointed at her friend, dousing her with an antiheadache spell and a feel-good booster. Both would wear off soon, but a good night or two of sleep would restore Valerie's health more than magic spells could.

Holding on to the Eight-Ball, Sabrina sped back to Mr. Copeland's office. She handed the Eight-Ball to Hilda, who promptly zapped it back into the copy of *The Discovery of Magic* Sabrina had taken it from.

Sabrina glanced at the watch, seeing it count down from nine seconds, eight seconds, seven seconds . . . "Can you get us back in six seconds?" she asked Zelda.

The minor tremor shook the ice rink again. "Done!" Zelda exclaimed wearily. "But moving that many people *and* a structure with pinpoint accuracy really wears you out."

Sabrina ran to the front doors again and peered outside. The familiar street scene greeted her eyes. They were back home.

"Hey, Sab," Harvey called from behind her. She turned to face him.

"Aren't you coming back to the dance?" Harvey asked. "I'm getting kinda lonely out there."

"Give me a minute," Sabrina said. "Valerie got sick and I'm helping her."

Worry darkened Harvey's features. "Need a hand?"

158

"I think I've got it. I'll be right with you." Sabrina stepped back into Mr. Copeland's office just as Zelda was unfreezing the man.

Mr. Copeland shook himself. "Wow. Must have had a brain freeze there for just a minute. I forgot what I was doing."

"You were telling us about the CNN show," Hilda answered, pointing at the television set. "They just figured out that the deep space probe's broadcasted signals must have overlapped Channel Eight's and made it look as if the Westbridge Harvest Moon Dance was being broadcast from one of Jupiter's moons." She winked at Sabrina, letting her know her aunts had fixed that as well.

"Yeah," the ice rink owner said. "That was it."

When Mr. Copeland's attention was on the television, Sabrina zapped up some aspirin and Pepto-Bismol equivalents. Then she took them to Valerie.

Valerie was already feeling better when Sabrina returned. Valerie was walking around the rink, freed from the effects of the Eight-Ball. "What did you do with it?" Valerie asked.

"It's gone," Sabrina promised. "You'll never see it again." She handed the medication over, then went to get Valerie a glass of juice from the caterer's table. Once she had her friend settled and relaxed, Sabrina joined Harvey out on the ice.

The music changed over to a slow, aching

ballad as Harvey took her hand. The light show techs dimmed the lighting and left only a soft electric blue arcing through the dark space that barely did more than lighten the shadows skating across the ice.

Monsters and aliens skated hand in hand with robots and movie characters.

"You know," Harvey said, "you were really right about this dance theme. With the skates and the light show, you could really almost believe we were on another world."

"Careful," Sabrina warned with a smile. "You never know. You could get exactly what you're asking for."

Harvey took her in his arms, guiding them toward the center of the rink where a single starry beam gleamed down onto the ice. "Would it matter?" he asked.

"And what if you ended up on a world filled with the most vicious creatures in the known galaxy?" Sabrina asked.

"As long as we're together," Harvey asked, "would it really matter?"

Sabrina looked deep into his smiling eyes. "Not to me," she answered. "Why don't you tell me that again. I really liked the sound of it."

Harvey held her close as he spun her under the gleaming star above. Then he whispered into her ear. "Where we go wouldn't matter to me at all, Sab. As long as we're together."

Sabrina hugged him tightly, then pulled away

and looked at him. "You never know, Harvey Kinkle, you might regret those words one of these days."

"No way," he told her.

And Sabrina truly believed him because she felt the same way.

About the Author

Mel Odom often wishes he had witch powers. They would make traffic jams easier to take (simply fly over them or zap home). They would make vacations easier (simply zap everybody there, then zap back for the things you forgot the first time!). And they would probably make getting chores done around the household easier to accomplish. (Haven't cleaned your room? Well, let's see how you like being a toad for the evening! Too busy primping to do your laundry? How would you like a *really* bad hair day?)

But he is grateful for the small magics that make life really good, friendships, dreams, and the fact that everybody in the family loves baby Chandler. He firmly believes the strongest magic in all the world is a baby's smile, which can melt the hardest of hearts and open doors everywhere.

He lives in Moore, Oklahoma, with his wife and five children, and leaves his Friday nights open to watch Sabrina with the family. He's written dozens of novels, including one in *The Secret World of Alex Mack* series called *In Hot Pursuit!* If you'd like to drop an e-mail to say hi, you can reach Mel at denimbyte@aol.com.

Win a trip to Hollywood!

to record your own CD in celebration of the official Sabrina soundtrack in the
"SABRINA SING-A-LONG SWEEPSTAKES!"

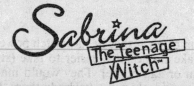

MUSIC FROM **SABRINA, THE TEENAGE WITCH** ON GEFFEN RECORDS

1 GRAND PRIZE

A trip for two (winner and chaperone) to Hollywood for a recording session sponsored by Geffen Records, Inc. Winner will also receive 25 copies of their recorded CD, a visit to the Sabrina, The Teenage Witch™ set at Paramount Pictures, and a "Sabrina, The Teenage Witch" licensed merchandise package.

☆ **See next page for exciting runner-up prizes!** ☆

Complete entry form and send to:
Pocket Books/"Sabrina Sing-A-Long Sweepstakes"
13th Floor, 1230 Avenue of the Americas, NY, NY 10020

Name_____Birthdate____/____/____

Address_____

City_____State/Province_____

Zip code/PC_____Phone (____)_____

5 FIRST PRIZES

A magical "Sabrina, The Teenage Witch" gift package featuring Archway Paperbacks' Sabrina, The Teenage Witch: Magic Handbook, Tiger Electronics' crystal ball and psychic telephone, Pastime Industries' craft kits, Geffen Records' "Sabrina, The Teenage Witch" soundtrack CD, and make-up from Cosrich all packed in a Honey Fashions "Sabrina, The Teenage Witch" backpack

10 SECOND PRIZES

A complete set of "Sabrina, The Teenage Witch" books from Archway Paperbacks published by Pocket Books and a "Sabrina, The Teenage Witch" soundtrack CD from Geffen Records, Inc.

15 THIRD PRIZES

A "Sabrina, The Teenage Witch" psychic telephone and crystal ball from Tiger Electronics and a "Sabrina, The Teenage Witch" soundtrack CD from Geffen Records, Inc.

25 FOURTH PRIZES

A "Sabrina, The Teenage Witch: Spellbound" CD-Rom adventure game from Simon & Schuster Interactive/Knowledge Adventure, Inc. and a "Sabrina, The Teenage Witch" soundtrack CD from Geffen Records, Inc.

50 FIFTH PRIZES

A one year "Sabrina, The Teenage Witch" subscription from Archie Comics and a "Sabrina, The Teenage Witch" soundtrack CD from Geffen Records, Inc.

100 SIXTH PRIZES

A "Sabrina, The Teenage Witch" soundtrack CD from Geffen Records, Inc.

Pocket Books/ "Sabrina Sing-A-Long Sweepstakes" Sponsors Official Rules:

1. No Purchase Necessary. Enter by mailing this completed Official Entry Form (no copies allowed) or by mailing a 3" x 5" card with your name and address, daytime telephone number and birthdate to the Pocket Books/ "Sabrina Sing-A-Long Sweepstakes", 1230 Avenue of the Americas, 13th Floor, NY, NY 10020. Entry forms are available in the back of Archway Paperbacks' Sabrina, The Teenage Witch: SABRINA GOES TO ROME and HARVEST MOON by Mel Odom and NOW YOU SEE HER , NOW YOU DON'T by Diana Gallagher, on in-store book displays, on the web site SimonSays.com and on coupons inside Geffen Records' CDs. Sweepstakes begins 9/8/98. Entries must be received by 12/31/98. Not responsible for lost, late, damaged, stolen, illegible, mutilated, incomplete, or misdirected or not delivered entries or mail or for typographical errors in the entry form or rules. Entries are void if they are in whole or in part illegible, incomplete or damaged. Enter as often as you wish, but each entry must be mailed separately. Winners will be selected at random from all eligible entries received in a drawing to be held on or about 2/1/99. Winners must be available to travel during the months of February and March1999. Winners will be notified by mail.

2. Prizes: One Grand Prize: A 3-day/2-night stay for two (winner and chaperone, chaperone must be winner's parent or legal guardian) to Hollywood including round-trip coach airfare from major U.S. airport nearest the winner's residence, round-trip transportation to and from airport, hotel accommodations and all meals. Winner will also receive a recording session sponsored by Geffen Records, Inc. 25 copies of their recorded CD, a visit to the "Sabrina, The Teenage Witch" set at Paramount Pictures, a "Sabrina, The Teenage Witch" gift package (from Archway Paperbacks, Cosrich, Geffen Records, Inc. Simon & Schuster Interactive/Knowledge Adventure, Inc and Tiger Electronics (approx. retail value: $2,500). Five First Prizes: A magical "Sabrina, The Teenage Witch" gift package with Archway Paperbacks' Sabrina, The Teenage Witch: Magic Handbook, Tiger Electronics' psychic telephone and crystal ball, Pastime Industries' craft kits, Geffen Records' "Sabrina, The Teenage Witch" soundtrack CD, and make-up from Cosrich all packed in a Honey Fashions "Sabrina, The Teenage Witch" backpack (approx. retail value: $120.00). Ten Second Prizes: A complete set of "Sabrina, The Teenage Witch" books from Archway Paperbacks published by Pocket Books and a "Sabrina, The Teenage Witch" soundtrack CD from Geffen Records, Inc. (approx. retail value: $95.00). Fifteen Third Prizes: a "Sabrina, The Teenage Witch" psychic telephone and crystal ball from Tiger Electronics and a "Sabrina, The Teenage Witch" soundtrack CD from Geffen Records, Inc. (approx. retail value: $70.00). Twenty-Five Fourth Prizes: a "Sabrina, The Teenage Witch: Spellbound" CD-Rom adventure game from SSI/Knowledge Adventure, Inc. and a "Sabrina, The Teenage Witch" soundtrack CD from Geffen Records, Inc. (approx. retail value: $45.00). Fifty Fifth Prizes: a one year subscription to "Sabrina, The Teenage Witch" comics from Archie Comics and a "Sabrina, The Teenage Witch" soundtrack CD from Geffen Records, Inc. (approx. retail value: $36.00). One Hundred Sixth Prizes: a "Sabrina, The Teenage Witch" soundtrack CD from Geffen Records, Inc. (approx. retail value: $15.00). The Grand Prize must be taken on the date specified by sponsors.

3. The sweepstakes is open to legal residents of the U.S. and Canada (excluding Quebec) ages 8-15 as of 12/31/98, except as set forth below. Proof of age is required to claim prize. Prizes will be awarded to the winner's parent or legal guardian. Void in Puerto Rico and wherever prohibited or restricted by law. All federal, state and local laws apply. Viacom International, Inc. Archie Comic Publications Inc., Geffen Records, Inc. and Universal Music and Video Distribution, Inc. their respective officers, directors, shareholders, employees, suppliers, parent, subsidiaries, affiliates, agencies, sponsors, participating retailers, and persons connected with the use, marketing or conduct of this sweepstakes are not eligible. Family members living in the same household as any of the individuals referred to in the preceding sentence are not eligible.

4. One prize per person or household. Prizes are not transferable and may not be substituted except by sponsors, in the event of prize unavailability, in which case a prize of equal or greater value will be awarded. Prizes are subject to production schedule and availability of talent. All prizes will be awarded. The odds of winning a prize depend upon the number of eligible entries received.

5. If a winner is a Canadian resident, then he/she must correctly answer a skill-based question administered by mail.

6. All expenses on receipt and use of prize including federal, state and local taxes are the sole responsibility of the winners. Winners will be notified by mail. Winners may be required to execute and return an Affidavit of Eligibility and Release and all other legal documents which the sweepstakes sponsor may require (including a W-9 tax form) within 15 days of attempted notification or an alternate winner will be selected. The Grand Prize Winner's travel companion will be required to execute a liability release form prior to ticketing.

7. Winners or winners' parents on winners' behalf agree to allow use of their names, photographs, likenesses, and entries for any advertising, promotion and publicity purposes without further compensation to or permission from the entrants, except where prohibited by law.

8. Winners agree that Viacom International, Inc., Archie Comic Publications Inc. and Geffen Records, Inc. and their respective officers, directors, shareholders, employees, suppliers, parent, subsidiaries, affiliates, agencies, sponsors, participating retailers, and persons connected with the use, marketing or conduct of this sweepstakes, shall have no responsibility or liability for injuries, losses or damages of any kind in connection with the collection, acceptance or use of the prizes awarded herein, or from participation in this promotion.

9. By participating in this sweepstakes, entrants agree to be bound by these rules and the decisions of the judges and sweepstakes sponsors, which are final in all matters relating to the sweepstakes. Failure to comply with the Official Rules may result in a disqualification of your entry and prohibition of any further participation in this sweepstakes.

10. The names of major winners will be posted at SimonSays.com (available after 2/1/99) or the names of the winners may be obtained by sending a stamped, self-addressed envelope to Prize Winners, Pocket Books "Sabrina Sing-A-Long Sweepstakes," 1230 Avenue of the Americas, 13th Floor, NY, NY 10020.

*Put a little magic in your
everyday life!*

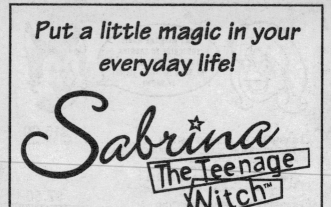

Magic Handbook

Patricia Barnes-Svarney

**Sabrina has a Magic Handbook, full of spells
and rules to help her learn to control her magic.
Now you can have your own Magic Handbook,
full of tricks and everyday experiments you
can do to find the magic that's inside and all
around you!**

Available mid-November

From Archway Paperbacks
Published by Pocket Books

2021